As if he knew what she was thinking, Sam leaned over and whispered, "Transformation happens very, very slowly. It takes centuries to become a full zombie."

That was supposed to make Megan feel better, but it didn't. "Centuries?" she gasped.

"You're immortal now," Sam told her. "Didn't anyone tell you that?"

She thought back to the things that she knew about zombies. She didn't recall Zach saying that she'd live forever. It wasn't on the websites she'd looked at either.

Megan would be twelve years old from now on. With no real friends at her new school, that didn't sound so good.

ROTTEN APPLE BOOKS

Mean Ghouls by Stacia Deutsch

Zombie Dog by Clare Hutton

MEAN GHOULS

by Stacia Deutsch

ROTTEN
APPLE

SCHOLASTIC INC.

New York   Toronto   London   Auckland
Sydney   Mexico City   New Delhi   Hong Kong

No part of this publication may be reproduced, stored
in a retrieval system, or transmitted in any form or
by any means, electronic, mechanical, photocopying,
recording, or otherwise, without written permission
of the publisher. For information regarding permission,
write to Scholastic Inc., Attention: Permissions
Department, 557 Broadway, New York, NY 10012.

ISBN 978-0-545-39823-7

12 11 10 9 8 7 6 5 4 3 2 1   12 13 14 15 16 17/0

Printed in the U.S.A.   40
First printing, August 2012

To my Good Ghouls: Abby, Izzy, and Lucy

CHAPTER ONE

"I've got zombitus," Megan Murry said. Her new cell phone felt warm and heavy in her hand. She'd hoped to get a phone for her thirteenth birthday, but that wasn't until next year. Getting the gift early was great, except that it was a pity present. Her parents felt sorry for her and wanted to do something "nice."

Sighing, Megan leaned back into the pillows on her bed and told Rachel, "It's a virus."

"Impossible," her best friend replied. "I've never heard of zombie-i-tus? I thought you had the flu."

"So did I!" Megan exclaimed. "Turns out that when your knees lock straight and you start to moan uncontrollably, it's not the flu at all. Mom and Dad took me to see a special doctor. Dr. Shelley did a bunch of tests and the results were all positive."

"No way!" Rachel was shocked. "Hang on, I'm Googling it." Megan could hear the clicking of Rachel's keyboard. "Ha! I knew it. No such thing as zombie-i-tus."

"Try again." Megan said. "It's not called zombeeee-i-tus. Plain zombitus. As in 'Bite us.'"

"Oh," Rachel said as Google reloaded. "I see it now." There was a long pause as Rachel read about the disease. Megan had already scanned through everything she could find online.

"Bummer," Rachel said at last. "Especially that part about how if you get a head wound it'll never heal. And that other part about how your skin might decay and fall off, that's bad, too."

"No kidding," Megan agreed. "It's totally gross. Dr. Shelley said that zombitus is going around, and it's super-contagious," Megan told Rachel. "All kids with the virus have to be quarantined in boarding schools. Apparently, there are Zombie Academy schools popping up all over the world. The doctor said I'm lucky there's one within a few hours of here. I can stay in Southern California and don't have to go to Australia. . . ." Her voice trailed off as she added, "Real lucky, I guess."

"I guess," Rachel echoed.

"Zach says that doctors at the Zombie Academies are looking for the cure."

Megan's eight-year-old brother was completely monster obsessed. When the pediatrician said she needed to see a specialist, Zach was the one who suggested that Megan see Dr. Rosemary Shelley because she was both a doctor and the author of his favorite book: *The A–Z Monster Encyclopedia.*

"Zach would know," Rachel agreed. "I bet he's seen every scary movie ever made."

"And now, he's making his own movie about —" Megan began, but Rachel interrupted.

"Hang on a sec, Meg. Doorbell."

With everything that had happened over the weekend, Megan had forgotten that the sixth grade theater club was meeting at the Hoffmans' house before school today. The cast was going to school early to hang posters for the show. Megan didn't do theater with Rachel. She played soccer instead.

Megan could hear Rachel chatting as she welcomed kids into her house. Megan's new phone was a basic model, but she didn't need video chat to imagine Rachel dressed for school in jeans and a T-shirt, her long bright red hair hanging straight down her back.

Megan's hair was as long as Rachel's, but where Rachel's hair was always neat, Megan's auburn mess was crazy curly and uncontrollable. Megan pulled it back in a ponytail, but it never stayed put. She'd always wanted hair like Rachel's —

"Zombitus?!" a boy exclaimed. "What's that?!"

"Shhhh," Rachel told him. "She's on the phone. She can *hear* you."

"Give me that," the boy said.

"No. It's mine." Megan listened to Rachel's laughter as she wrestled to keep her cell.

After a long minute, the boy announced with a snicker, "You lose!" Then, cheerfully, he said, "Hiya, Megan," into the receiver.

Megan immediately recognized Brett Hansen's voice because she was a Brett Hansen expert. It was embarrassing, really. She'd read Brett's online profile so many times she had it memorized. School pictures usually stunk, but Brett's photo was amazing. His crew-cut hair was so dark it glowed against the beige background. And his new wire-framed glasses were awesome; they made his head look round like a pumpkin. A supercute pumpkin.

Megan didn't have any classes with Brett, but she had math with his twin sister, Hailey. Hailey was popular and fashionable . . . and mean to anyone who wasn't popular and fashionable. Once, when Megan wore a shirt that Hailey called "ugly," one of Hailey's friends spilled Kool-Aid on her at lunch. Megan couldn't prove it wasn't an accident, but right after that, Hailey winked and waved.

Since then, Megan avoided Hailey and her friends as much as she could.

Brett wasn't like Hailey at all. It was hard to believe they were related.

"Hi," Megan said in a very small voice.

"Hey," Brett said. "Just wanted to say thanks."

"For what?" Megan managed to ask. She didn't know what he was talking about.

"I didn't have cash on Friday and I was starved. Since you weren't at school, Rachel said I could *borrow* the leftover half of the brownie in your locker." He smacked his lips. "I left an IOU. When you get back to school, I'll buy you something at the snack bar. Anything you want."

"Um. Okay." Megan imagined them standing in line together. Brett made her nervous so she usually avoided talking to him. She didn't want to say something wrong. Hopefully, the snack-bar line would be extra-short that day.

"So what's this bizarr-o virus you have?" Brett asked.

"Um . . ." Megan didn't know how to explain in just a few short words, so she didn't reply at all.

In the background, Megan could hear Rachel's mother offering the kids bagels with cream cheese and orange juice.

"Megan?" Brett's mouth was obviously full of bagel. He swallowed hard, then shouted into the phone. "You there? Megan!?" Then, "Did I drop the call?"

"Give back my phone!" Rachel grabbed her cell back from Brett.

"Megan?"

"Yeah, I'm here."

Rachel whispered into the phone, "Don't be so self-conscious. Brett's easy to talk to." Then she laughed. "It cracks me up that your crush is playing my crush in the school play."

Megan joined in Rachel's laughter at her awkwardness. "I hope I'm back in time to see it. . . ." Her voice trailed off. Then Megan said softly, "Someone from the zombie school is coming to get me soon. I better go finish packing."

Rachel's voice softened as she began to realize that Megan was really leaving Dana Point. "Can I call you there?"

"Call. E-mail. Write letters." Megan hoped she'd get news from Rachel every day. "You have to keep me informed about the play!"

"You mean about Brett," Rachel said with a little giggle.

"Maybe," Megan admitted. "Just tell me everything that happens at school, okay? Even if you think it's boring, I want to know."

"I promise." There was a long pause of heavy silence before Rachel said, "Well, bye, then."

"Yeah," Megan said with a deep, sad sigh. "See ya."

Rachel hung up.

Megan crashed back into the pillows on her bed. She hated zombitus and hated leaving Dana Point Middle School. She covered her head with a pillow and moaned, "Uhhhh-uhhhh." She also hated that she couldn't stop making that sound.

"The call of the undead," Zach whispered in a ghostly voice. "Music to my ears."

Megan popped up. "Where'd you come from?" she asked.

"The hall," Zach replied, pointing over his shoulder with his thumb. "Duh."

Megan slapped Zach with a pillow. "You know what I mean, dork."

Zach laughed. "Don't tackle the guy who's risking his life to bring you breakfast." He pointed at a loaded tray on her desk, then brushed his hair off his forehead. Everyone said that Zach's straight brown hair and football-player build came from Mrs. Murry's side of the family, while Megan's insane curls and string-bean legs came from her dad's.

Megan walked over to the tray, even though she wasn't hungry at all. Suddenly, she turned to face her brother. "Hey!" she exclaimed. "You're not wearing your sanitary gear!"

"Mom and Dad are terrible hall guards. Besides, I'm not scared of catching the disease," Zach said. "Honestly, I'm kinda jealous. I mean, I'm the one who loves monsters and yet, you get to be one."

Megan reached back, swooped the pillow off the floor, and smacked him with it again. "I'll trade. You can be the zombie," she said.

"I have a better idea." Zach puckered and made smacking sounds. "Since the disease is contagious, if you kiss me, I can come with you."

"You really are a dork," Megan said, shaking her head. "Mom and Dad need you here. I'll get better and come back soon." Crossing her fingers as she glanced at her breakfast, Megan hoped it was true.

The tray was covered with a paper towel. Megan lifted it and gasped. The stuff on the plate looked disgusting. Pink and lumpy. "What is this?" She turned to her brother.

Zach raised his eyebrows. "Brains, of course."

"No . . ." Megan was horrified.

"I just wanted to help you adapt," Zach told her. Laughing, he admitted, "It's spaghetti. With blush sauce and sausage links."

That didn't sound so bad, but Megan turned it down.

"There's more." Zach told her to look under the upside-down drinking cup. Beneath it were some moldy blueberries. They'd grown white fuzzy fur and were stuck together like a big lump.

"I knew you'd like the dessert." He winked. "Spoiled fruit is a zombie favorite."

She still wasn't hungry, but weirdly the rotten berries really did look yummy. Zombitus had some very strange symptoms! Megan grabbed a spoon and ate all the blueberries in one big gulp. They were delicious. "Thanks," she told Zach.

"Megan!" Mrs. Murry called from downstairs. "Your ride's here."

Megan looked out her bedroom window. A long black limousine was parked in the driveway. A painted banner on the side said ZA TRANSPORT.

"Zombie Academy." Megan rolled the name of her new school around on her tongue. "Dana Point Middle School" sounded better.

"Tell Zach to get out of your room!" Mr. Murry shouted up the stairwell. "We know he's in there."

"He needs to put on his protective mask and gloves," her mom added.

"They might not be good hall guards," Megan said, "but they are good parents." She grinned.

"Eyes in the back of their heads," Zach agreed. "There isn't even a monster name for that kind of vision." He grabbed a bag that he'd set down by the door when he came in. "I have presents for your trip."

"More presents?" The pity phone from their parents would be hard to beat.

Megan took Zach's sack and opened it. Inside were some balloons he'd made from Dr. Shelley's protective gloves. He'd decorated a few germ-preventing face masks, each with a different monster sneer or grin. And there was a strangely shaped key on a chain.

"A skeleton key," Zach said with a laugh. "A necessity for every monster!"

"Skeleton?" Megan put the key around her neck as Zach explained how it could open any lock.

Megan had no clue how the key could be useful, but the name *was* funny. "Thanks," she said as she reached in to take the last thing out of the bag.

Stuffed in the bottom, Megan found a T-shirt that said EVIL GENIUS across the front.

"This is your favorite shirt," Megan said. She tried to give it back to him.

"I know it won't fit you, but maybe you could pin it to the wall or something," Zach said, leaping forward and hugging his sister tight. He buried his head in her shoulder. "I'll miss you."

"I'm gonna miss you, too, dork," Megan said and held her brother until the limo driver honked.

It was time to go.

CHAPTER TWO

The ride to Zombie Academy was the longest two hours of Megan's life.

When she arrived at the front gate, the first thing she saw was a very cute boy her own age. He had dark skin, thick brown hair, and wore jeans with a white T-shirt and a sweater vest. The glassy look in his eyes might have been a symptom of zombitus, or it might have been that the boy just played a lot of video games. It was impossible for Megan to tell the difference.

For a moment Megan wondered if she was at the right school.

"Hi. I'm Sam," the boy greeted her.

"Hi." Megan went to shake his hand but as she touched him, his thumb fell off. It wasn't bloody or gross. It simply dropped to the dirt like a loose button or a bit of lint.

"Oh, uh . . ." She grimaced, glancing between his four-fingered hand and the thumb. She had no clue what she should do. "I'm sorry," Megan said at last.

"No problem." Sam quickly picked his thumb up and blew off the dust. "I lose parts all the time. The nurse sews them back on for me. We've tried every kind of thread. Nothing holds very well." He pulled a small Ziploc baggie out of his pocket and showed Megan his pinky toe. "Might as well get two digits done at the same time." He put his thumb in the bag and then stuffed it into his pocket.

Sam thanked the limo driver. Megan hadn't looked at the man before; she'd only seen the back of his head while he drove. And now she was glad she hadn't looked. His head was barely attached to his neck. It kept lolling over to one side or the other. One of his eyes was hanging loosely from some kind of oozing stringy stuff. And though she hadn't noticed it from the backseat, *whew*, the guy stunk!

It was impossible to imagine how he'd driven the car safely. If her parents had seen him, they'd never have let Megan in the limo. No wonder he'd kept the tinted windows rolled up and shouted, "Get in!" to

Megan. She was glad to have arrived safely and relieved when the limo drove off, leaving her on the sidewalk with Sam.

While Sam got her suitcase, Megan grabbed her backpack. It was then that Megan finally took a good look around.

Zombie Academy was straight out of one of Zach's horror movies: a castle nestled among the trees, with a high fence and a huge iron gate surrounding the complex. Megan wondered if the gate kept healthy people out or the zombie kids in. She didn't really want to know the answer.

The castle itself was made of stone. It was pretty, but also a place you'd expect to be haunted. Or infested by the living dead. There was a tower on each side of the gate, and small slit windows. Megan thought she saw some girls peeking out of one of the windows, but when she squinted for a better look, they were gone.

"Come on," Sam told Megan. "The outside of the school is kind of spooky, but the inside has been totally redone. A long time ago this millionaire, Lewis Jones, got the zombitus virus and decided to spend all his money looking for a cure. When other people got infected, he invited them to come to his estate. Then, he went around the world to find known zombies and invited them to come here, too. Mr. Jones pays for everything." Sam added, "Of course, once the researchers find the antidote, the deal is he gets the first shot."

"What about the other Zombie Academies?" Megan asked.

"Yep, he built those, too," Sam said. "You'll meet Mr. Jones later. He's like a grandfather to everyone who lives here."

Sam let Megan in through the gate, then locked it behind her.

She gave him a puzzled look.

"I've been here a long time," he explained. "I like to help out. When I heard you were coming, I offered to come meet you. There's no one who knows their way around this place better than me. Except Mr. Jones, of course." Sam led her into the main part of the castle. "So, Megan Murry, welcome to Zombie Academy."

"Whoa." Megan was amazed. The interior of the building really didn't match the outside. The halls were filled with beautiful museum-quality paintings and sculptures, modern lighting, leafy tropical plants, and, in the middle of the entry, a glass elevator that led to the higher floors. It reminded Megan of a hotel her family had stayed at on a vacation to Hawaii once. There was even a small waterfall flowing into a koi pond.

"Come on." Sam set his four-fingered hand on Megan's back and led her into the elevator. "Level five is the dormitory. I'll show you your room. Then you need to check in at the nurse's office. She'll give you your class schedule." He patted his pocket. "We can go together."

"The girls in the dorm room next to yours are mean. Really mean." Sam grimaced as they walked by a purple-painted door decorated with three cutout gold stars. Each star had a name on it: Brooke. Betsy. Brenda.

"'Zom-Bs,'" Megan read the big letters printed above the names.

"My advice," Sam said, "is to ignore them. Fly under their radar. The Bs are nasty."

Megan thought about Brett's sister, Hailey Hansen, and her gang of mean girls. "Gotcha," Megan told Sam. "I know girls like that at home."

"We all do," Sam said with a sigh.

He knocked on a plain brown wooden door. "Home, sweet home."

The girl who answered the door wore a black dress with black shoes and tights. Her hair was dyed black. Her eyeliner was black and so was her eye shadow. Even her lipstick was black. She looked like a vampire, not like someone with zombitus.

"Hey-ya, Happy," Sam said as if the girl's appearance was totally normal. "Do any painting today?"

Happy didn't seem very happy. She sulked across the room and turned an easel to show Sam a fresh canvas.

"Finished it," she said in a voice that sounded like Eyore from *Winnie the Pooh*.

The painting was, well, black. Completely black to the edges of the canvas.

"Wow!" Sam exclaimed. "That's one of your best!"

Happy moaned. "It's not very good."

Sam turned to Megan. "Picasso had his blue stage. Happy's in a darker phase."

"I call this one *Midnight*," Happy explained.

Megan could see how the title fit. "It's . . . pretty," she said.

"Thanks," Happy muttered, stepping away from the canvas. She pointed to a twin bed on the other side of the room. "That's yours. The mattress is lumpy."

Megan could have guessed which bed was hers. It had white sheets and yellow covers, whereas the other bed . . . all black.

"I'm sure it will be comfortable," Megan said, trying to stay upbeat.

"No," Happy replied. "It won't."

Megan let out a huge sigh. She assured herself everything would be okay. Zach had told her that zombies didn't sleep much, anyway.

"Well," Sam said, "you two can get to know each other later. Megan and I have an appointment with Nurse Karen."

"Nice to meet you," Happy said in a way that made Megan think she didn't mean it.

"Yeah," Megan replied. Happy wasn't anything like Rachel, but Megan didn't have any friends at Zombie Academy. She needed to be nice to Happy. Maybe there was a smile hidden under all that dark face paint. "Want to have lunch together?" Megan asked.

Happy pinched her lips, considering Megan's invitation. "Okay. But the cafeteria food isn't like what you're used to at home."

Megan knew about moldy fruit already, but had a pressing question. "We don't really have to eat brains, do we?"

"On Mondays they serve last year's vegetables," Happy said. "I'll meet you in the dining room at noon."

Spoiled vegetables. That wasn't too bad. And yet, Megan was left to wonder what was on the menu for Tuesday.

CHAPTER THREE

"I like Happy," Sam told Megan as they walked back to the elevator for a trip to the second floor. "Unfortunate name, though."

Megan gave a small laugh. She hoped Sam would be her friend, too.

The nurse's office was in the same long hallway as most of the classrooms. The waiting room was packed. There was a boy of about six whose eyeball had fallen out during first-grade circle time. The kids in the classroom were still looking for it. Next to him sat a teenage girl whose teeth had suddenly sharpened overnight. She'd accidentally bitten her tongue. Three other kids had gashes that were oozing thick, goopy blood.

In the corner, Megan spotted a teacher. She was young, blond, and very pretty. Megan noticed that her legs were locked straight, forcing her to lean against the wall like a wooden plank.

"Mine were like that," Megan said. "But they got better." She smiled encouragingly.

"I've been like this for a week," the teacher replied. "My knees won't bend, no matter how hard I try."

Megan shivered. She looked around the room and wondered if this was her future. Would Brett talk to her if she had to carry her eyeball around in a Baggie? Would Rachel want to hang out if Megan had those razor-sharp teeth? What if she could never, ever, play soccer again?

As if he knew what she was thinking, Sam leaned over and whispered, "Transformation happens very, very slowly. Bit by bit. It takes centuries to become a full zombie."

That was supposed to make Megan feel better, but it didn't. "Centuries?" she gasped.

"You're immortal now," Sam told her. "Didn't anyone tell you that?"

She thought back to the things that she knew about zombies. She didn't recall Zach saying that she'd live forever. It wasn't on the websites she'd looked at either.

Megan would be twelve years old from now on. With no real friends at her new school, that didn't sound so good.

"That's not going to happen!" Megan said. "I'm not going to be immortal, because Mr. Jones and his researchers are looking for a cure. I'll be home in a few weeks. Maybe a month, right?"

Sam got a distant look in those glassy eyes and said, "Sure, Megan. You'll be going home soon."

"Hang on, Sam. How long have you —" Megan began to ask but was interrupted by the nurse calling her name. Her questions would have to wait.

She gave Sam a long last stare, then went into the examination room with Nurse Karen.

The nurse was a fully transformed zombie. No question about that. Her green eyes were glued open, her cheeks sunken. Megan tried not to stare at the double row of shark-sharp teeth that gleamed at her.

Everyone at the school had the disease, but it was like Sam said — there were different stages of transformation.

The nurse had Megan do a few jumping jacks and some squats. Then she had her read a page from a college textbook aloud and answer some questions.

Megan felt like she did okay. She moaned between every paragraph, but otherwise she read the text just fine. It was about cars, and since her dad was a car salesman, she had an advantage and answered the questions easily.

Next Nurse Karen asked Megan to count to one hundred. No problem.

And then, she asked the exact same reading comprehension questions again.

This time the questions were harder to answer. Megan felt like she'd read the passage a long time ago, and struggled to remember what it said.

"Good work," Nurse Karen said after Megan finished. She took out a graph that charted the zombie transformation time line and held it up. Megan noticed that Nurse Karen's fingernails were bruised black-and-blue. "So, here's where you are." She pointed to the very beginning of the chart and traced an arrow with one finger. "And here's a zombie." Megan wanted to plug her ears and run away, but she took a deep breath and listened.

"Decay happens slowly, and you're still at the very beginning of the process."

That seemed like good news.

"Do you want me to describe what you might expect over the next couple hundred years?" Nurse Karen asked.

"No!" Megan said so quickly she thought she sounded rude. "I mean, I saw the kids in the waiting room. I've got an idea of what will happen."

Nurse Karen nodded and handed Megan a white slip of wrinkled, torn paper that had her schedule on it. "Sam will escort you today. He's in many of your classes." The nurse also gave Megan a spiral notebook with ZOMBIE ACADEMY printed in bright red letters across the front.

"Thanks," Megan said. Dana Point Middle School didn't give out notebooks for free. The students had to buy them.

"This will help you remember things," the nurse explained. "I encourage all my patients to write *everything* down." She gave Megan a whole box of new pens.

"Oh," Megan said, handing back the spiral. "I don't need a notebook. I have a good memory."

"Trust me. You'll need it." Nurse Karen opened a drawer. Inside there were laptops, phones, electronic organizers, and used notebooks. "Memory loss is a side effect of the transformation," she said. "Hang on to the notebook. Everyone seems to forget their things around here."

"Got it," Megan said, thinking about what happened with the reading comprehension questions. She took the notebook. "I'll write everything down." Megan gave Nurse Karen a small smile, even though she felt like screaming.

Nurse Karen also offered a warning. "Try your best to stay calm, Megan. Zombitus transformation happens more quickly when you're emotional. You should avoid getting upset or angry if you can."

Megan nodded. "Got it," she said again. "Nurse Karen?" There was one last thing Megan needed to know. She'd keep asking it over and over until someone gave her the answer. "When are they going to find a zombitus cure?"

Nurse Karen acted as if she hadn't heard the question. "Can you please send Sam in? I think we'll try superglue on him this time."

Megan was sitting on a bench in the waiting room next to a girl who couldn't stop moaning, when Sam came out of Nurse Karen's exam room. Megan jumped up. "What's the deal with the cure?"

Sam wiggled his thumb, checking it. "I don't —" he started.

"Tell me the truth," Megan barreled on. "I thought I was only going to be here a little while. The doctors are working on a cure, right?"

"Yes. They are," Sam said softly, taking Megan's elbow and hustling her out of the waiting room. "Are you sure you want to know?"

Megan thought that was an odd question. "Of course I do," she replied.

Sam nodded. "A few days ago, Mr. Jones announced that they'd found a zombitus cure."

Megan was thrilled. This was great news. She'd be home even sooner than she thought. "So where is it? When can I get some?"

Sam led Megan down the hall. "Trials are starting next week."

He didn't seem nearly as happy about it as Megan would have expected. She also wondered why the nurse hadn't mentioned it when Megan asked, but *WHATEVER*!

"So I'll only be here a little while more?" It was terrific news! The best!

"Mr. Jones gets first stab," Sam said, not even

smiling at his own pun. "Then I suppose they'll start with the kids who have been here the longest."

That meant Sam would get his really soon. Why wasn't he jumping up and down? Megan sure felt like she wanted to.

Her arms suddenly popped out in front of her in a traditional zombie walking pose. It only lasted a second. That was a new symptom.

Megan rubbed her elbows and said, "I'm the newest, so I'll be last." She thought about it some more and declared, "Last is better than never."

"I guess." Sam stepped into the classroom. "But while we're waiting to be cured, we have math class."

CHAPTER FOUR

There was a crowd in the main hallway.

"Uhhhh-uhhhh." The kids passing from room to room sounded like a moaning symphony.

"Is it always like this?" Megan asked Sam, shouting above the racket.

"Always," Sam replied in a loud voice. "You'll get used to it." Just then, Sam let out a huge "Uhhhh."

"If you can't beat them," Megan said with a laugh, "join them."

As they worked their way through the crowd, Megan saw a girl drop a piece of paper. The girl didn't notice. She kept on walking, the frills of her fancy blue dress swishing as she continued down the hallway.

"Hey, wait!" Megan called out. "You dropped your —"

The hallway was so packed and the groaning so loud, the girl couldn't possibly hear her. "No worries," Megan said to herself as she bent to get the paper. "I'll get it." By the time she stood up and looked around, the girl was gone.

"What's that?" Sam asked, eyeing the page in Megan's hand.

"I don't know," Megan said. She looked down to see loopy handwriting on yellowed stationery that was crinkled at the edges as if it had been read over and over again. "It's a letter from someone's mom," she reported to Sam. "I'm sure whoever it belongs to would want it back. E-mail is fine, but I love getting real mail."

"Tell me who it's to," Sam said. "It'll be easy to return. I know everyone."

Megan was careful not to read the letter — that would be rude. She only checked the beginning and the ending. *"Dear Gertrude.'"* And *"Love, Mom.'"*

"Who's Gertrude?" Sam asked.

"I thought you knew everyone," Megan countered with a wink.

Sam shrugged. "So did I."

"I got this one covered," Megan said. "I saw who dropped it." Megan held the page carefully so she wouldn't add any more creases.

As they reached the classroom, three girls huddled in front of the door, whispering to one another.

The girl who dropped the letter was Asian with short dark hair cut in a bob. Her oversize cobalt blue prom dress might have been nice if someone hadn't run over it repeatedly with a car. There was an obvious tire track down the back, mud splatters covered the satin skirt, and deep tears ran across the frilly front. She also had an oozing neck wound, which she attempted to cover with a silk floral scarf.

Megan rushed forward. "Gertrude?" The girl didn't turn around, so Megan tapped her on the shoulder and shouted over the moans echoing through the hall. "Gertrude?"

A few kids nearby quieted down and stared at Megan with wide eyes.

The girl turned to face Megan. Her friends stood beside her, no longer in a tight circle, but in an imposing line, like a wall.

"You're Gertrude, right?" Megan held out the letter.

"No." She looked at the letter, but didn't reach out to take it.

"But, I —" Megan was confused. She'd seen this girl drop it. Her memory seemed fine. She felt one hundred percent certain she had the right person.

"She *said* that's not her name." A blond, super-thin girl with skin so white it was see-through stepped forward.

"But —"

"It's not her name!" The veins in this girl's arms popped red and blue as she put her hands on her hips.

Megan looked at the letter. "So, are you Gertrude?" she asked.

Some of the kids in the hallway began to snicker. Megan could hear the name "Gertrude" whispered over and over as if it was the funniest thing anyone had ever heard.

"I'm Brooke," the pale girl said. "And you're making a big mistake."

"Oh." Megan squinted her eyes at the third girl.

"Don't even think about it." She pushed her palm in Megan's face like a stop sign. "I'm Betsy." Betsy had caramel-colored skin, and was pretty enough to be a model. In fact, she reminded Megan of a very popular, gorgeous pop star from Mexico. Unfortunately, Betsy's light brown hair was thinning and her eyes were all white, with no pupils. She'd have a hard time getting a runway job looking like that.

Turning back to the first girl, Megan said, "Then it *must* be yours. I saw you drop your letter, Gertrude. Don't you want it back?"

"I'm Brenda," she sneered.

Brooke, Brenda, Betsy — these were the Bs who lived next door to her and Happy. Sam had warned her to stay away, so she pulled back the letter. If Gertrude wanted to call herself Brenda, who was she to argue? "Okay, then, sorry to have interrupted you. I'll just take this to Mr. Jones and leave it —"

Brenda's hand shot out and snagged the letter from Megan. She ripped it away so forcefully that a tiny piece of the corner tore off. Opening her palm, Brenda waited for Megan to hand over the torn shred. Then she carefully tucked the letter into her binder.

Jeers and cheers of "Gertrude, Gertrude, Gertude" filled the hallway.

Brenda spun around, scanning the students, fire in her eyes. "If anyone ever, ever calls me that . . . they will be very sorry." She glared at Megan. "My name is *Brenda*."

Brenda gathered her friends close and the three of them turned and stormed into the math classroom. The door slammed shut, leaving Sam and Megan in the hallway.

"Wow," Sam said. "Your first day at school and you've already annoyed the Mean Ghouls. Good work." Sam opened the door to let Megan inside the room. "Most people take a lot longer to get their attention."

"I thought I was doing a good thing," Megan said, feeling baffled by what had just happened. "And what's with the name Mean Ghouls? I thought they called themselves the Zom-Bs." She felt sure that if Zach were here, he'd give Sam and Megan a long lecture on the intricate differences between ghouls and zombies.

"I call them Mean Ghouls because that's what they are. They dubbed themselves the Zom-Bs when they realized that all of their names start with a *B*." Sam showed Megan where to sit and plopped into the desk next to her. "Brenda must have picked a new first name when she came to ZA." He paused before saying, "Zom-G just doesn't have the same ring."

"Yikes." Megan was glad that she was with Sam at the front of the room, while the Mean Ghouls sat in the last row. She glanced over her shoulder and was met by three Ghouls casting nasty looks at her.

She quickly looked away.

"We still on for lunch?" Happy asked Megan as she sat down at the desk on Megan's other side. Happy must not have heard what had happened out in the hallway . . . yet. She set out her ZA notebook and opened to a blank page.

"Definitely," Megan replied. If Happy hadn't heard about the "incident" by lunch, Megan would fill her in. "So, what are we working on?" she asked. It was strange joining a class that had already started. "Algebra? Geometry?"

Happy flipped back through her pages. "Hmm, I can't really remember." She squished up her face and pressed her black lips together. "Something with numbers," she said. "Does it really matter?"

"I suppose not," Megan replied.

"Let us begin." Mr. Hornsby, the math teacher, picked up a piece of chalk. He had a huge gash in his head that revealed his brains. Megan was surprised that brains actually did look like the spaghetti that Zach had made for her last breakfast at home. A pink slime coated with gray, thick linking twists. Disgusting! Each time Megan looked at him, her stomach flipped over. Staring at her desk, she fiddled with her pen and doodled in her notebook — anything to avoid looking up.

"Please pass out the textbooks," Mr. Hornsby told Brenda.

"I can't," Brenda replied. "I don't know where they are."

Nurse Karen hadn't been kidding about zombitus causing memory loss. But it seemed random, like some stuff was easier to remember than other stuff. Brenda recognized the letter from her mom and her real name, but didn't have a clue where the math books were kept.

Megan's own brain felt foggy, but so far she hadn't forgotten anything. At least, she didn't think she had.

Mr. Hornsby checked his own red Zombie Academy notebook, then sent Brenda to the cabinet in the back of the room.

Brenda took her time delivering books around the room. When she got to Sam, she tossed a book onto his desk at just the right angle for it to slip over the side and onto the floor.

"Oops," she said with a snicker.

Then she turned to Megan, who held out her hands. But Brenda hadn't forgotten *everything*. She flung a book at Megan's head and sneered, "Welcome to Zombie Academy, New Girl."

Megan's soccer reflexes kicked in just in time. She ducked, then popped under the heavy text, bobbling it on top of her head like a soccer ball. With a little bounce, she heaved it up and caught it in her hands.

"Thanks," Megan said with a wink.

"Uhhhh," Brenda growled as she turned to the next desk.

"Mean Ghouls," Megan said to Sam. It was about how they acted, not whether they ate brains. "I get it."

"More than *mean*. Brenda just tried to crack your skull," Happy told Megan.

"You're right!" Megan suddenly realized what Happy meant. Rachel had read on the zombitus website that zombie head wounds don't heal. If Megan hadn't been so quick, the corner of the heavy textbook would have given her a gaping, brain-revealing wound. She looked at Mr. Hornsby's head and shuddered.

"Thank you, Brenda," Mr. Hornsby said when all the books were passed out.

Megan guessed he hadn't noticed Brenda throwing the book, so she raised her hand to report it.

"Yes . . ." Mr. Hornsby checked his notebook, searching for her name. "Megan."

Quickly glancing over her shoulder, Megan saw Brenda whisper something to Brooke and Betsy. They all giggled.

The scene felt way too familiar. It reminded her of the way Hailey Hansen and her friends acted back home.

Feeling like she'd already started enough trouble, Megan decided that she'd stay away from the Ghouls from now on, like Sam had suggested.

Megan lowered her hand. "Forget it," she told Mr. Hornsby.

Which he immediately did.

With an "Uhhhh-uhhhh" groan of her own, Megan opened her book to chapter two.

*   *   *

When math was over, it was time for English. The class was taught by the teacher Megan had met at the nurse's office, the one with the knee-locked legs. Her name was Mrs. Yarrow and she leaned against the wall while she lectured the class. She was interesting, and a dramatic storyteller. Rachel would love her. Megan was preoccupied with thoughts of home until Mrs. Yarrow mentioned their new assignment five minutes before the end of class.

"A woman named Mary Shelley wrote the book *Frankenstein* in 1818. It's the story of a man who creates a monster. There are copies on my desk. Please take one and read chapters one through five for homework. When we meet on Wednesday, we will be discussing the question, *Is the Frankenstein monster a zombie?*"

The bell rang and Megan checked her schedule. She had PE next.

Sam showed her where the locker rooms were, and once they'd both changed, they headed out to the ball field. Megan soon realized that PE at Zombie Academy was anything but typical.

About half of the kids in the class couldn't bend their knees. A few had their arms stuck straight out and couldn't lower them. She'd never seen so many bloody wounds, at least not *before* a game.

Taking a scrunchie out of her pocket, Megan tied back her mop of hair. She bent her knees to make sure they weren't stuck and jogged in place to warm up.

The coach was another fully transformed zombie.

"He played in the Olympics," Sam told her.

"Cool." Megan asked which year and sport.

"776 BCE," Sam replied, pausing for Megan's jaw to drop. "He was a wrestler."

"You have to be kidding." Megan checked out the coach, who looked to be about thirty years old. He was bald, with patchy places on his arms where his bulging muscles stuck out through the skin. "I'm supposed to believe that he's more than twenty-five hundred years old?" Megan asked. "No way." She shook her head.

"Zombies are immortal," Sam reminded her. "He's the same age now as when he got the disease. Coach Ipthos was haunting Mount Olympus, scaring tourists, when Mr. Jones invited him to teach here."

"This is all very strange," Megan said, letting out a long breath.

"Come on. Follow me." Using a hand-drawn map, Sam helped Megan dodge around several deep holes dug in the field.

Coach Ipthos divided the kids into teams and then — threw out soccer balls.

"Soccer!" Megan was excited.

"Kind of," Sam said. "We call it shuffle ball."

Megan and Sam were on opposite teams. He grinned, challenging her to show what she could do.

"If this is anything like soccer . . ." Megan muttered to herself, checking out the field. "He has no idea who he's up against."

The game was similar with a few new rules.

No bending knees. Even if you could, bending was a penalty. That gave the players who couldn't bend a chance.

The deep holes in the field were traps. If you fell in, you were out. Coach would rescue the fallen players at halftime so they could rejoin the game.

The holes added a fun obstacle since five seconds after being rescued, most kids couldn't remember where the traps were and fell right back into them.

Megan wondered why Happy wasn't at PE, but when the whistle blew, she pushed that thought aside and went for the ball.

Turned out, Sam was as good a player as Megan. Maybe better, but she'd never tell him that!

As if the holes weren't enough, the Bs made the game even more difficult. They refused to get sweaty so they didn't play. But rather than waiting on the sidelines, the three of them stood in the center of the field, blocking the way for both teams.

Sam said that Coach Ipthos liked adding another obstacle to the game so he never forced them to play.

When Megan got near, Brenda and Brooke each took turns trying to trip her. Betsy, it turned out, had a cleanliness obsession and wouldn't do anything that might get stains on her clothing. "If anyone oozes zombie goop on me, I'll kill them!" she shouted any time a player got too close.

Avoiding the Bs, Megan and Sam dueled it out near the sidelines. By the end of class, Megan's team had narrowly won, 3-2.

"That was fun!" Megan hurried down the field. She went to give Sam a high five, but he kept his hands behind his back.

She thought he was being a sore loser until he said, "Smacking is a bad idea. I'll lose a finger for sure." Sam grinned and very carefully put his hand out for a loose shake instead. "Good game."

Megan lightly touched his hand.

"Let's go." Sam immediately closed his fingers around hers and held on. "This way." He took out his map and led Megan around the deep field traps and into school.

When they reached the locker rooms, Megan was reluctant to let go.

"See you at lunch," Sam told her, casually breaking the hold.

"Okay," Megan replied, glancing down at her warm, empty palm.

As he went into the boys' locker rooms to change for lunch, Megan headed to the girls' and quickly searched her backpack for her cell phone. She checked the time. "Darn." Rachel was in class.

Not wanting to forget, Megan made a note in her spiral to call Rachel later.

She couldn't wait to tell her best friend all about Sam.

CHAPTER FIVE

The next morning, something was nagging at Megan's memory.

Something important she'd forgotten.

She opened her notebook. There were only two things listed.

Read *Frankenstein*.

Check. She'd done that and taken careful notes.

Next: Call Rachel.

Check. She'd done that last night before bed.

Rachel had wanted to know if she still had a crush on Brett. And for a second Megan couldn't remember who Brett was, so she looked him up online and pasted a printout of his profile page in her notebook.

Of course she still had a crush on Brett. She'd liked him since she'd met him.

Sam was — well, Megan didn't exactly know what Sam was.

"He's a new friend," Megan told Rachel. Which was true.

That's when Rachel said, "Brett's been asking about you."

"Really?" Megan's heart felt like it might leap out of her chest. "When?"

"He asks at least once every day," Rachel told Megan. "Sometimes when we eat lunch together or when we hang outside during free period, and almost always after school when I see him at the theater."

"Wow," Megan said. "Brett is asking about me. Very cool."

"Yeah," Rachel said. "He is cool."

That night Megan stayed up, smiling to herself, reading and rereading Brett Hansen's school profile.

In the morning she told herself that when she got back to Dana Point, she'd go by the school theater first thing and talk to Brett. Really talk to him, looking him in the eye and everything.

Megan checked her notebook again. Calling Rachel wasn't what she'd forgotten.

"I seriously have to write *everything* down," Megan told herself. It felt like her zombitus brain fuzz was slowly getting worse. Then again, if she had to have symptoms, brain fog was better than peeling skin.

The calendar said it was Tuesday. Megan reviewed her schedule.

The day before, when Megan met Happy for "lunch," she'd discovered a pretty great thing about Zombie Academy: There were no classes after noon! It wasn't perfectly perfect because she had three classes on Monday, Wednesday, and Friday, and another three on Tuesday, Thursday, and SATURDAY! But still, since her afternoons were free, Megan didn't mind too much that her Saturdays were school days.

After classes ended today, she was going with Sam and Happy to the school movie theater. They were showing zombie movies, of course. If zombitus wasn't contagious, Zach really would have loved this place!

Thinking about Zach made Megan think about her parents. And about Rachel.

She missed them all so much. She'd only been gone a night and yet it felt like much longer. It was hard to say if that was the creeping zombie brain fog, or just normal homesickness.

Thankfully, when the cure was released, she'd get some and then . . .

THAT'S IT!

The cure was the thing she'd forgotten.

She wanted to find out more about it. Plan her trip home. Tell Zach, her parents, and Rachel.

Of all the things to forget, Megan couldn't believe *that* was the one that slipped out of her brain.

Before calling her parents, she needed information. Like when EXACTLY she'd be leaving. Sam seemed to know everything about ZA, so she'd ask him. Thankful that her knees could bend, Megan ran all the way to her first Tuesday class. It was Zombie History.

"Sam!" she shouted as she rushed into Room 601. "I need to know —"

The classroom was full. It was the biggest room in the castle and every zombie in the school was packed in tight. Teachers, staff, and students —

everyone. The moaning was so loud and constant, it sounded to Megan as if she'd walked into a beehive.

Sam and Happy were sitting together on the floor.

"Excuse me." Megan had to step over several straight legs to reach them. While she was picking her way toward her friends, someone shoved her from behind. "Umph," Megan said, as she turned to see who'd pushed her.

Brooke gave Megan a sharp-toothed smile. "Not sorry," she said.

Brenda and Betsy sneered.

"Not-apology not accepted," Megan replied.

She'd watched the Bs in the school hallways and around the dorm. They were mean. And yet everyone wanted to hang out with them, to dress and act like them. Kids looked up to them and did what they said to do. Popularity was confusing.

Megan gave Brooke her very own normal-toothed smile and took a seat on the floor, squishing herself in between Happy and Sam.

"It's hot," Happy said. "This place is crammed with too many people."

Megan had to agree. "What's going on? Is Zombie History always this crowded?"

"Class got canceled," Sam whispered to Megan as the lights suddenly dimmed. "Didn't you get the announcement?"

Megan shook her head. She glanced up and saw Brenda holding a bright red piece of ZA stationery in the air. Megan's name was printed across the front in big letters. While Megan watched, Brenda ripped it into tiny shreds and threw the confetti pieces into the air. They drifted down like bloodstained snowfall.

"Ugh." Megan turned away.

A spotlight illuminated the front of the classroom.

"Teachers, children, and friends..." The man who stepped into the light was the fattest zombie Megan had ever seen. He'd stopped aging at about forty and wore Bermuda shorts and a Hawaiian shirt, with a lei of fresh flowers around his scratched, fleshy neck.

"Let me guess." Megan leaned over to whisper to Happy. "Mr. Jones?" He fit right in with the decoration of the Academy. He'd created a tropical paradise for his permanent vacation.

"He has terrible taste in fashion," Happy replied.

Megan looked at Happy's own outfit. She was wearing black pants today, instead of a black skirt.

But it was still all black, all the time. Megan wasn't convinced Happy was a fashion expert.

Mr. Jones was drooling blood. Wet, soggy bloodstains covered the front of his shirt. Megan hoped it was his blood. If he'd snacked on someone else's brains, she was outta there, contagious or not. Megan shivered.

"It's okay," Sam told her. "Mr. Jones is very nice. You should go see him. He likes to meet new students."

Megan didn't feel comforted. She wrapped her arms around her bent knees and shivered again. "'Did you say 'meet' or 'eat' new students?" Megan asked Sam.

Sam laughed. "Stop worrying. Mr. Jones doesn't eat kids. Go see him. He lives behind the school. There are signs pointing the way."

Megan said she'd think about it. Then she wrote a reminder down in her notebook so she wouldn't forget.

"I have called you all together for a reason," the owner of the castle said loudly. Mr. Jones paused a long minute to let the zombies get out their groans. When the room settled, he went on. "As you know, our researchers here at the ZA California Castle have discovered a cure for zombitus."

The room erupted in thin applause. Megan clapped louder than anyone.

"I know you are eagerly anticipating the cure." He wiped at his mouth with a white handkerchief, smearing blood across his chin.

To calm her nerves, Megan told herself that he'd probably been eating strawberry Jell-O in the hallway and focused on the fact that she was about to find out the one thing she really wanted to know. With excited anticipation, Megan leaned forward.

"I have waited many years, centuries even, for this day," Mr. Jones said. His voice had a slight tinge of a European accent. As if he'd lived in California a very long time, but had originally come from somewhere else.

Mr. Jones scanned the crowd and took a deep breath before casting his eyes downward. "I regret to inform you that last night our lab was broken into." He paused for another round of moans. "The cure was stolen."

CHAPTER SIX

Megan was devastated. "But, but, but . . ." She couldn't wrap her brain around the idea that she wasn't going to be home in a few days. A big tear rolled down her cheek.

"Don't get too emotional," Happy warned. "Remember what Nurse Karen said?"

Megan actually did remember. "Zombitus gets worse if you get mad or angry."

"Or sad or scared," Happy added. "Or feel too happy."

"Right." Megan sniffed back her tears.

Happy handed Megan a black handkerchief. "This is just like last time."

"Exactly," Sam said as they walked together to science class.

Megan wiped her eyes and asked, "Last time? What do you mean?"

"Since I've been here, it's the third time this has happened," Sam said.

Happy said, "Someone doesn't want us to be cured."

"Whoever it was took all the notes, fried the computers, and trashed the lab." Sam repeated what Mr. Jones had told them in the meeting. "The doctors will have to start again."

Megan blinked back more tears. "Can't they remember what they did?"

"They all have zombitus, too. Their memories are fuzzy," Happy said as she pressed the button for the glass elevator. The science lab was on the third floor. "No one can remember all the steps to make the cure."

"Don't they have ZA notebooks?" Megan held up the one Nurse Karen had given her. It simply wasn't possible that the cure was gone.

"You heard Mr. Jones. They were stolen," Sam said, shaking his head. "They're going to have to start all over again." He frowned. "From the very beginning."

"But they'll find another cure?" Megan asked, struggling to stay positive. "Won't they?"

"Someday," Happy assured her in a voice that was not very convincing. She added, "I hope you like it here, Megan. Looks like we're all gonna be here a long, long time."

Megan couldn't focus in science and this time she was sure it wasn't because of zombie brain fog. She was sad, mad, and homesick. She didn't want to be at Zombie Academy for "a long, long time." All Megan wanted was to go home, back to her normal life.

She was so preoccupied that she didn't see someone rush by her desk toward the supply closet. And she didn't notice when that same zombie returned, this time pausing to add something red to the slimy blue molecular solution Megan had been working on all period.

Unfortunately, she didn't clue in until the experiment turned bright purple and began to bubble over, spilling across the table and onto the floor. It burned a large hole through the desk and dissolved the floor tiles near Megan's feet.

The smell was horrible!

And to make things worse, Dr. Verma made Megan put on protective gear and get a mop, even though the mess totally wasn't her fault! But it didn't matter who caused it, the experiment was Megan's responsibility.

Through the visor on the thick rubber face mask, Megan could see the Bs gathered together at the back of the room. She hadn't seen which one did it, but Megan knew the Ghouls were behind the chemical attack.

Brooke, Betsy, and Brenda were acting busy. Brooke was managing the lab work, writing in a red pen that matched her see-through veins. Brenda was retying the bow on her green prom dress, similarly frilly to yesterday's — but also torn and dirty with tire tracks down the front. And Betsy was washing her hands with sanitizing lotion.

"Megan, come here for a moment." Dr. Verma had won a Nobel Prize in chemistry before she contracted zombitus. She was part of the school's research team. And she had no sense of humor. "You did not follow the experiment's instructions," she said in a heavy Indian accent. "And you've ruined school property. Can you explain yourself?"

"I —" Megan began to explain, but since she hadn't seen the Bs actually do anything, she felt uncomfortable blaming them. Even if she was positive they'd caused the damage.

"Yes?" Dr. Verma asked.

"I guess I made a mistake." Megan lowered her head.

She got a zero on the lab.

The Mean Ghouls giggled to one another, but Megan didn't care.

Her parents would be mad when they heard she wasn't doing well in science. And still, Megan didn't care.

Megan didn't care about anything. It had been a horrible morning. All she wanted to do was go back to her dorm room, curl up in bed, and cry. Instead, she had to sit on her stool and wait for the others to wrap up their lab experiments.

Class still wasn't over when Happy raised her hand. "Dr. Verma, Megan got some chemical slime on herself."

Megan looked down and sure enough, whatever the Ghouls had added to her test tube was rapidly eating through the front of Megan's T-shirt. There was a hole revealing Megan's belly button, and if she didn't change fast, the acid would destroy her entire shirt.

Happy quickly got permission to go with Megan back to the dorm. Out in the hall, Happy surveyed the damage. The hole was spreading up toward Megan's neck. "Lame Ghouls," Happy groaned. "We don't have time to go all the way to our room." The bathroom was nearby, and the girls ducked inside. "You have to get that thing off now."

Megan jumped into a stall and pulled off the remnants of her acid-eaten top. "What am I going to wear?"

Happy opened her backpack and pulled out a shirt. She threw it over the stall door to Megan. Megan could barely contain her surprise as she pulled it over her head.

The shirt was totally cute. It was bright blue with small yellow flowers hand-sewn on the shoulders. And nothing on it was black.

"I love this!" Megan told Happy.

"I hate it," Happy replied. "I was going to throw it away."

"Where'd you get it?" Megan asked as she tucked the shirt into her jeans.

"I made it," Happy said.

"Huh?!" Megan was shocked.

Happy gave a heavy sigh as she admitted, "I sew."

Megan came out and admired her reflection in the mirror. "You're really talented."

"I don't think so," Happy replied. Very carefully, she picked Megan's old shirt off the floor, where it was burning a hole in the tile beside the toilet, and threw it away. The chemicals immediately began to dissolve the metal can as white, wispy smoke filled the bathroom. "Your shirt is eating the castle. We gotta take care of this before we go back to class."

Megan waited while Happy called for a janitor.

A fully transformed zombie woman, dressed in an oversize Hawaiian muumuu, arrived within seconds. She put the whole can inside the stainless-steel hazardous waste cart she'd brought with her.

Happy said, "Mahalo," Hawaiian for *thanks*, and the woman disappeared as fast as she'd arrived.

Once again, Megan felt like she was a guest at a resort hotel. She wondered if drinks would be served with tiny umbrellas. Of course, she might never know the answer. Zombies rarely got thirsty.

After the trash can was gone, Happy explained, "My parents are fashion designers." She paused then said, "They're kind of famous." Happy blushed and pointed to herself. "My whole name is Henrietta Alicia Paulette Patricia Yeverman."

"Yeverman!" Megan knew that name. "Wow." She looked at Happy in a new way. Her roommate was rich — very, very rich — and connected to celebrities. And, she *was* a fashion expert. Megan felt bad for doubting her.

"Close your eyes before they fall out," Happy said with a scowl. "Don't make me regret telling you. I don't want people here to know." She groaned. "I told my parents they are *not* invited to Visitors' Day."

Whoa! Megan didn't know what was more surprising: Happy was the daughter of famous fashion designers. Happy could sew — in color. Or that there was a Visitors' Day!

One thing at a time. "Why black?" she asked as Happy slicked on a fresh coat of dark lipstick.

"I want to be different," Happy replied in a thin voice. "Everyone here gets a fresh start. Didn't you change anything about yourself when you left your last school?"

"Uh, no." Megan had no idea what Happy was talking about. "Change what?"

Happy turned to Megan. "You said Brenda changed her name from Gertrude, right?" Megan had told Happy about the hallway incident the day before while they ate decayed zucchini casserole for lunch. "Now, take Brooke for another example. We went to the same middle school in New York. She was the least popular girl there."

"Seriously?" Megan asked. She tried to imagine Brooke without the Bs.

"She got here, found the Bs, and" — Happy smacked her lips together — "with a little work on her nasty attitude, ta-dah, she's popular." Happy slid the lipstick back into her bag and added, "Those other Bs weren't the queens at their old schools either."

"Hmmm." Megan thought about what she was like at her middle school in Dana Point. She was pretty quiet. And she tended to avoid confrontation with mean girls like Brett's sister, Hailey. It hadn't occurred to her to try to be more popular or to change who she was when she got to ZA. But she did feel stronger here. And less likely to take orders from anyone just because they were popular.

"And you?" Megan asked Happy. "How did you change?"

"My parents expect me to design clothes and someday work with them — so that's what I used to focus on. I never painted before I got here," Happy admitted. "I like it."

Megan smiled. It was the first time she'd ever heard Happy say anything positive.

Of course, being Happy, she immediately added, "I'm not very good, though."

"Sam thinks you're great," Megan said. "Why not try painting in color?"

"Boring." Happy snorted. "Then I'd be like everyone else."

As they walked out of the bathroom, Megan found that she was feeling a little better. She still wanted to get cured and go home ASAP, but now that Happy had shared something private, something really important to her, she felt like she had a best friend at ZA.

And she was fascinated by the idea that kids coming to the Academy felt like they could change who they'd been or how they'd been treated at their old schools. Megan wondered about Sam. What had he been like before? Was he different now, too?

"Home economics is starting now." Happy looked at her watch. "Science is over."

"Isn't home ec a thing from the 1950s?" Megan asked.

That wasn't what she'd planned to ask Happy. She had a different, more important question to get to first, but yet again, the thought wasn't sticky in her brain. It was frustrating not being able to remember what you were thinking minute to minute.

"In the olden days, home ec used to be for girls to learn sewing, cooking, cleaning — you know, the skills they'd need when they got married." The corners of Happy's lips rose to the place where Megan thought she might smile. But she didn't. "Now it's about living a zombie life."

"I don't get it," Megan said. "A zombie life?"

"It's an easy class." Happy checked her red notebook for the schedule. "Today, we're cooking zombie food."

"That doesn't sound bad," Megan said. "I liked the cafeteria vegeta —" It took an instant for Megan to realize what they were making. "Ugh. We're doing brain recipes, aren't we?" Megan's stomach flipped as if she'd just gotten off a roller coaster. "Ewww," she said.

"Don't worry," Happy said. "We don't use real human brains in class. You can choose rabbit or pig."

"Uhhhh-uhhhh," Megan groaned. She thought she might puke.

Even without smiling, Happy could joke. "Just kidding," she said dryly. "We're making desserts out of rotten fruit."

Suddenly, Megan's stomach felt better, and she found she was in fact hungry. "I could go for that."

"I hate fruit," Happy said. "And vegetables. And meat. And bread." She added, "And brains."

"Of course you do," Megan said with a chuckle, adding, "I hate brains, too."

As they walked down the hallway, a young boy, about ten years old, came rushing up to Megan. He grabbed her around the waist so hard, he nearly knocked her down.

"I love you," the boy said. He had straight dark hair and wore glasses. There was a huge gash over one of his eyes and a long gooey slash down his right arm. If she ignored the zombie stuff, the boy reminded Megan of Zach.

"Uhhhh," Megan half groaned. She wasn't sure how to respond. It was the first time a boy, other than her dad, had told her he loved her.

He released her from the hug, just enough to look up at Megan. "Until you came, the Bs didn't like me because I pulled a fire-alarm prank that made the sprinklers go off in the dorm and got all their stuff wet!" He hugged Megan again. "They've been mad at me for years. But now they don't like *you* more." Megan cringed. She hadn't meant to make them hate her.

The class bell rang and the boy said, "You saved my zombie-life." He stood on tiptoes and kissed Megan's cheek before running off to join his friends.

"I can't believe the Mean Ghouls would pick on a little kid." Megan turned to Happy. "If the Bs can change from unpopular to popular, I wonder what it would take to change them back." She bit the inside of her cheek, then, realizing if she made a sore it might never heal, stopped.

"I can only think of one way to knock them down," Happy replied. The Bs were standing at the end of the hallway, staring at Megan.

Megan knew what that one thing was.

She had to find the missing zombitus cure and send the Bs back to the middle schools they came from.

CHAPTER SEVEN

Sam was her partner in home ec. They were making a pie out of rotten strawberries with moldy tomatoes and overripe avocados. As the smells of the spoiled fruit wafted through the air, Megan found herself drooling.

"We have to cook it first," Sam said as Megan popped a furry green strawberry into her mouth and moaned.

"Just making sure the strawberries are safe," Megan said, tipping her head over her shoulder at the Bs. "I hear the Ghouls have a plot to poison you."

"Funny." Sam laughed. "It's not me they are after." He added with a wink, "New Girl."

Megan frowned. "True."

"Sorry for how things turned out." Sam said. "I warned you when you got here, but maybe I should have been more specific. Or defended you in some way."

"It's okay." Megan picked up a bowl and began to smash the strawberries into a thick pulp. "I can handle myself."

"All you have to do is hang in there," Sam said. "Eventually they'll forget about you. Or sooner or later someone newer than you is bound to do something they think is worse than giving Gertrude back her letter."

Megan didn't like that thought. She'd rather take on the Bs than pass them off to another kid.

Looking over her shoulder, Megan noticed that Happy was paired with Brooke. They were chatting as they both scooped avocado from the skin. Megan felt a little like Happy was hanging with the enemy, but Mr. Franko, the home ec teacher, had chosen the pairs.

Mr. Franko was the only teacher on staff who wasn't a zombie. He'd been a TV chef on a reality show until the entire cast got the virus. For some reason, Mr. Franko was immune. He came to ZA with his staff, who were all now employed at the castle. "The researchers have been testing Mr. Franko to understand why he hasn't gotten the disease," Sam explained.

"Maybe Mr. Franko is part of the cure?" Megan asked. "He might remember what tests they ran on him."

Sam shrugged.

"Oh!" Megan remembered what she'd forgotten in the bathroom with Happy. "What about Visitors' Day?" She asked the question quickly so she wouldn't forget it again.

"What do you mean?" Sam looked at her blankly.

"When is it?" Megan asked. "I can't wait for you to meet my mom and dad and my best friend, Rachel." Every name made Megan more and more excited. Going home would be better, but having them come visit was pretty good. "Zach is going to love coming here."

"I don't know when it is," Sam admitted. "I don't invite anyone anymore."

Megan stopped crushing strawberries. "Why not?"

"No one's around for me to invite," Sam said in a monotone that made him sound like Happy. "You should go introduce yourself to Mr. Jones. He can tell you when it is."

Megan hadn't made an appointment because she was nervous to meet him.

"After class," she said, steeling her courage. "I'll go see him right after class."

"I thought we were going to the movies today," Sam reminded her. Sam's memory was much better than Megan's. She never saw him pull out his note-book to double-check things.

"I'll meet you at the theater," she told Sam. "Tell Happy to save me a seat."

Megan glanced back at Happy one last time. She was chatting with all the Bs now. It was strange. . . . Happy seemed . . . sorta happy.

At noon, classes were over for the day.

Megan decided that if she didn't go to Mr. Jones's bungalow right away, she never would. So after making a note to herself to go to the movie theater when she was through, Megan headed down the stone path behind the school, following the signs to Mr. Jones's house.

She hadn't been behind the school before. Since

she'd arrived the day before, she actually hadn't been outside. There were only three buildings on the ZA property: the castle; Mr. Jones's home, which was also his office; and the research center.

Mr. Jones's bungalow sat straight ahead of her, and through the trees to the right, she could see the red bricks of the center.

She meant to go straight, and yet, at the cross-roads, Megan found herself turning down the side path toward the research facility.

The castle may have been centuries old, but the research center looked brand-new. There were tall windows across the front, and a slanted roof that glowed as solar panels collected sunlight. Sam had told her that the doctors had the best technology available at their fingertips.

Her curiosity took her up to the front door. Megan was surprised to find it was locked. Yes, there *had* been a theft the day before. But shouldn't the doctors be back at work, trying to re-create the cure? She tried the buzzer, but no one answered.

"Hmmm." A few answers. That's all she wanted. If she could help find the missing vials of the cure, then maybe she could go home. But it was going to be hard if she didn't know what she was looking for.

Standing on the front stoop, Megan felt her legs begin to get heavy. Her right leg dragged as she staggered around the back of the center.

To her surprise, the back of the building was made entirely of glass. It was gorgeous. Megan imagined Dr. Verma standing in one of the sparkling new laboratories. In her vision, Dr. Verma took notes as she peered through a microscope. And when she got stuck on a problem — she would look out the huge windows to the forested area behind for inspiration. Maybe a deer or a bunny would wander by. And if no one attacked them to eat their brains, maybe the animals would begin to stop by for visits.

Megan was about to go back to the main pathway and try the buzzer again when she heard a loud metallic-sounding crash and a few raised — and very agitated — voices.

"Hello —" she began, hoping she might be let in for a tour. "I —" Megan became very quiet as she realized that she recognized those voices.

The Bs!

Frantically, Megan looked for a place to hide. She shuffled away from the building and ducked behind a thick cluster of pines.

Through the sharp, twisted needles, Megan could

see them. Brenda, Brooke, and Betsy crawled out of a broken window on the far side of the building.

"Uhhhh —" Megan threw herself to the ground and choked back the rest of her groan.

"Who's out there?" Brenda shouted. "Betsy, go look."

"I'm not going into the trees," Betsy said. "There are bugs and creepy things and," she gasped, "dirt!"

"This is no time to get hung up on cleanliness!" Brenda said. "Brooke, go take a look. I definitely heard something."

"I don't think that's such a good idea," Brooke said. She pointed to a nasty cut on her own forehead. "I already have to explain to my parents how I got this gash. My dad warned me that head wounds don't heal. He's not going to be happy."

"If you'd been paying attention, the cabinet wouldn't have fallen," Brenda spat.

"Betsy knocked it over," Brooke retorted.

"If you'd let me turn on a light, I'd have been able to see," Betsy said. "You know it's hard to see clearly without pupils!"

"Wear your glasses!" Brenda replied.

"They've been broken for a month," Betsy said. "You stepped on them in your high heels!"

"You left them on the floor," Brenda said.

"You knocked them off my face when your arms popped straight out," Betsy argued. "I'm waiting for a new pair. They have to be made special."

If Megan could have laughed without making a sound, she would have. The girls were acting like clowns. They couldn't stop bickering and nagging one another. And although Brenda thought she was in charge, it was obvious that Brooke and Betsy were getting tired of following her orders.

"Stop this nonsense," Brenda said sternly. "There isn't much time. We have to be ready on Visitors' Day."

"That gives us twelve whole days," Brooke said after counting on her fingers. "No problem." She touched her head. The cut was small, but deep, and a sliver of her brain was slowly oozing out. Brooke used a tissue to push it back inside her skull. Betsy gave her disgusted look and handed her a tube of hand sanitizer.

Cupping her ear and tilting her head toward the woods, Brenda listened hard. "I guess there's nothing out there. Let's go back to the castle. We'll finalize our plans at midnight on Friday at the meeting spot."

"I'll make sure Yeverman is there," Brooke said.

Betsy had a moment of zombitus memory loss. "Remind me, where's the meeting place again?"

"The tower," Brenda replied, pointing back toward the school. Then she turned to Brooke and asked, "Did you get what we need?"

Brooke held up a brown cloth sack. "I have them."

Megan could hear glass clinking in the bag as Brooke gave it a little shake.

"Careful with those," Betsy warned. "We're going to use them all!"

"This will be the best Visitors' Day ever," Brenda cheered. "Afterward, no one will care that the cure was stolen." The Bs high-fived one another, then rushed off toward the Zombie Academy castle.

The instant they were gone, Megan took out her ZA notebook. She wrote down everything she wanted to remember.

SUSPECTS	CLUES
Brooke	Visitors' Day
Brenda	Tower
Betsy	Glass in a bag

Bs meeting Friday night!!!

At the bottom of the page Megan wrote one last thing:

Happy Yeverman — how is she involved???

Megan didn't understand why Happy would be meeting the Bs on Friday at midnight. What were the Bs up to? And what did all of this have to do with the missing zombitus cure?

She looked at the page in her notebook and felt like that detective. The girl who solved crimes. The one in the books. In the movie. The girl with the boyfriend . . . Fred? Red? Ned. Yes. Ned.

What was her name? Thinking about it was giving Megan a headache.

On the way around the research center, the answer finally came to her.

Megan felt like Nancy Drew.

CHAPTER EIGHT

Thanks to the Bs, Megan knew when Visitors' Day was, so she didn't have to go see Mr. Jones. It was twelve days away. That meant Megan should invite her parents for the following Sunday!

Megan hurried back to the dorms to call her family.

Her dragging leg slowed her down and tired her out. By the time Megan reached her room, she was exhausted. Flopping back on her lumpy bed, Megan took a few breaths before dialing home.

Zach answered.

"Hey, dork," Megan greeted. "Mom there?"

"Duh!" he said. "It's only afternoon. She's still at work."

Megan checked the clock. Dad was probably at work, too.

"Don't you want to talk to me?" Zach asked, sounding hurt. "I want to hear all about the school and the zombies and the brains and the —"

"You can check all that stuff out for yourself," she told her brother. "Come a week from Sunday. It's Visitors' Day."

"OOOOHHHHH. Zombie Academy! Do we have to wear protective gloves and masks?"

Megan could hear the excitement rising in Zach's voice. "Probably," she said.

Zach paused. "I don't mind. It's worth it. Can I meet Mr. Jones?"

"How do you know about him?" Megan asked.

"I've been reading about your disease and the school," Zach told her. "Did you know Mr. Jones opened the California Castle in 1908?"

"I had no idea it was *that* old," Megan admitted. She started to do the math to figure out how old Mr. Jones must be, but Zach's mind was leaping at rocket speed. "Dr. Shelley might want to come to visit, too. I mean, she diagnosed your disease *and* wrote a book about monsters. Can I bring her? Can I? Can I?" He interrupted her thoughts.

"Sure," Megan agreed, just to get him to stop. Dr. Shelley was very old and had long gray hair.

"We can pretend she's our grandmother if anyone asks."

"Awesome!" Zach told her he was going to write a scene for his movie that took place at the school and bring his video camera. "What time should we be there?" Zach asked.

Megan checked her notebook. Maybe she should have gone to Mr. Jones after all. . . . She didn't know. "Just come in the morning and stay all day."

"Cool!" Zach said. He rattled off an itinerary for his day on campus, and plans for shots he wanted to get on video. Megan wasn't sure who was more excited about Visitors' Day, her or her brother. She was about to hang up when Zach asked, "Have you met any kids who like being zombies?"

"What are you talking about?" Megan replied. "Who'd *want* to be a zombie?"

"When I was reading about the school, it said that some people like having zombitus and don't want to be cured. I just wondered if you met anyone like that."

"Of course not," Megan said. "That would be crazy." Zach really was monster obsessed. She didn't feel like talking to him anymore. "Tell Mom and Dad to come next Sunday."

"Save me some brain soup," Zach said as he hung up.

Megan called Rachel next.

She'd just told her about Visitors' Day when Rachel asked, "Did you hear about Brett?"

"Hear what?" Megan didn't know what Rachel was talking about.

"You'll see," Rachel said, then fell silent.

"See what?"

Rachel didn't answer.

"Does everything have to be a mystery?" Megan asked. "Come on. Tell me the news."

"To-mor-row," Rachel said, stressing each syllable.

"Oh, fine." Megan gave up. "I'll wait, but you have to come to Visitors' Day next Sunday."

Megan could hear Rachel's smile through the phone. "You couldn't keep me away," Rachel said.

"Megan Murry, please come to the nurse's office."

Megan hadn't even known the school had an intercom system. Her name rang out and echoed down the hall.

"You'd better get going," Happy said. "It's irritating. They'll keep calling you over and over until you answer. Just in case you've forgotten your own name."

"Got it." Megan rushed to the elevator.

It was Wednesday. Rachel had said *something* would happen today. Something about Brett Hansen. Maybe there was a package for her — from Brett. Megan had been waiting all morning to find out what was going on.

It wasn't a package from Brett.

It *was* Brett.

He was standing in the nurse's office, holding a ZA notebook in one hand and a schedule in the other.

"Hi," Megan said, talking directly to Brett for the first time without feeling nervous at all. She didn't even stare at her feet. Instead, she gazed directly into his eyes. They were bloodshot and the pupils were bright red. Other than that, he looked cute as ever. She was glad to see him. Really glad.

"Megan," Nurse Karen said. "I hope you're willing to show our newest student around school."

Megan nodded enthusiastically. "Of course," she said. Brett Hansen! She couldn't believe that he went to ZA now, too. And it looked like his class schedule matched hers. Awesome!

"It's time for PE," Megan told Brett. She was surprised at how hard it had been to talk to him in Dana Point and how easy it was here. "You're going to love shuffle ball." She began to explain the rules to him, but soon Megan noticed that Brett still hadn't said anything. She waved a hand in front of his eyes. Brett just stared straight ahead into the distance.

They were still in the nurse's office so Megan rushed back to talk to Nurse Karen. "What's his deal?" she asked.

"Brett's transition is moving much faster than yours," the nurse explained. "He's in zombitus shock. Give him a few days. It usually goes away on its own."

Megan nodded and went back out to where she'd left Brett.

"Come on," she told him. "If Coach Ipthos can't shake your shock, we'll figure out something else."

Sam was waiting for Megan in front of the locker rooms.

Megan's heartbeat sped up a bit when she saw him, but then she remembered Brett. Brett was her . . . real life. When zombitus was finally cured, she and Brett would be going back to Dana Point and Sam would go to Seattle. Megan probably wouldn't see Sam ever again.

That made her a little sad, but it also convinced her that she needed to focus on Brett and helping him adjust to life at ZA.

"Who's this?" Sam asked.

"This is my friend Brett, from back home," Megan said. "He's got zombitus shock."

Brett couldn't shake Sam's hand, which was probably for the best since Megan worried about Sam's fingers.

"Zombitus shock?" Sam asked. "I haven't seen a case of that since nineteen —" He stopped himself midsentence. "Let's get him onto the field," Sam said quickly. "He needs fresh air."

"I'll go change. Meet you outside. Prepare to be beaten."

"Monday was beginner's luck," Sam replied with a snort. "Today, my team's going to kill yours."

"Kill us? You can't kill zombies!" Megan laughed. Sam chuckled.

"Uhhhh-uhhhh." Poor Brett stood there, moaning madly, staring straight ahead, unaware of the bad comedy routine taking place around him.

"I'll take care of your friend," Sam told Megan, suddenly serious. "We'll get him sorted out."

"Thanks," Megan said, her smile fading. She stood quietly, watching as Sam grabbed a second pair of shorts from his pack and led Brett toward the locker room to change clothes.

But Brett couldn't move. His knees were stuck, and so was his brain. He shuffled around for a second, then fell into a hole. And that was before the game even began.

Coach Ipthos suggested Brett join the Bs in the center of the field. "They don't play, anyways," he said with a groan.

Megan wasn't sure that was such a good idea. If Megan was playing ball, she couldn't protect him from Brenda, Brooke, and Betsy. And he was in no condition to protect himself.

"Hurry up!" Coach called to Megan, blowing his whistle. "Game's on."

With Brett standing next to the Bs, Megan couldn't focus. She kept narrowly avoiding falling into the holes, letting Sam score twice. At the half, while Coach pulled the kids out of traps, Megan went to check on Brett.

"Hi, Megan," Brett said as she got close.

Whew. He didn't seem to have any more symptoms

of the zombitus shock. Megan was relieved. "Feeling better?" she asked.

He couldn't bend his knees and one of his front teeth was supersharp, but his eyes weren't red anymore and everything else appeared normal.

"I made friends," Brett said, putting one arm around Brooke and another around Betsy, while Brenda stood to the side grinning.

"We think he's great!" Brenda smirked.

Megan was confused. "What are you up to? Are you tricking him?" Megan wouldn't let the Bs be mean to Brett.

Brenda laughed and rolled her eyes.

"Brett's cool," Brenda said. She was wearing a dirty pink prom dress that made her look like a poofy mud-crusted cupcake. "Cooler than you, that's for sure."

Brett laughed. "Lucky for me, my name starts with a *B*!"

"Uh, Brett, can I talk to you a second?" Megan was going to tell him he should stay away from the Ghouls, just like Sam had warned her on her first day. She'd remind him that he was a nice guy. He liked theater. He had a mini wiener dog named Fluffy. (She'd read that on his profile.)

"I'm a Zom-B!" Brett laughed hard, in a sharp way that sounded an awful lot like his twin sister, Hailey. "And the Bs don't like you." He raised his hand and waved. "Bye-bye."

"Great," Megan muttered as she turned and walked away. "Just rotten peachy."

Now, more than ever, she needed to find the missing cure. It was the only way to get rid of the Bs once and for all. She was going to sneak into that meeting Friday at midnight in the tower, discover what they were up to, find the cure, and save Brett before it was too late.

CHAPTER NINE

Nancy Drew had sidekicks. Megan found that out on a quick trip to the school library. She reread the first few novels and took careful notes on how to do detective work. Sidekicks seemed to be the most important part of the job. Very few detectives solved mysteries by themselves.

Determined to get some help, Megan went to find her friends.

Sam was sitting with Happy in the big, empty lunchroom, scarfing down what was left of the home ec pie. Megan could smell the rotten strawberries as she entered the room. They smelled so good that she nearly forgot why she was there. "The Bs are up to no good," Megan blurted.

"That's not new news," Happy said. She was sucking avocado mush out of her fingernails. "Tell us something we don't already know."

"I think they stole the zombitus cure," Megan said, pulling up a chair and sitting down.

"Well, that's something," Happy admitted. "Do you have proof, Sherlock?"

Sherlock . . . Megan was pretty certain that was the name of another detective. She'd have to go back to the library later to refresh her memory.

If Happy was involved with the Bs, Megan shouldn't really say anything, but since she didn't know for sure, she barreled on. "I saw them coming out of the research center. They were talking about the cure and doing something on Visitors' Day." She opened her notebook to get the facts straight. "They're having a big meeting Friday night."

Happy choked on a bit of avocado. "Really?" she asked. "A meeting?"

Megan couldn't stand sitting at the table watching them eat. "Can I have some of that?" she asked Sam before telling them her plan.

Sam passed the nearly empty pie dish. Megan took the last fingerful of the spoiled fruity dessert and stuffed it in her mouth. "Yum." She wiped her face on her sleeve.

"Never thought rotten fruit would taste so good, did you?" Happy asked.

"Never," Megan admitted. "About Friday . . ."

"I'm in," Sam said. "We can snoop around and see what they're up to."

Happy sighed. "I guess if you're both going, I'll go, too. Not like I have anything better to do that night."

Megan was encouraged. Whatever she'd heard at the research center was wrong. She could cross Happy's name out of her notebook. Happy wasn't going to be plotting with the Bs in the castle tower. She'd be spying on them instead.

The pie was gone, so Megan picked up the dish and licked the plate clean. Grinning, she said, "We're going to sneak around, so we should all wear black." There was a bit of strawberry mush on Megan's nose.

Sam reached forward to wipe it off with a napkin. Megan flinched but didn't back away.

"Clean," he reported when he was done. Then Sam turned to Happy. "Got anything thieving black I can borrow?"

"No," Happy told him.

She didn't seem to be joking, but honestly Megan couldn't tell.

Without saying bye, Happy got up and left the cafeteria.

When she was gone, Sam reached into his backpack. "I got you a present."

Megan raised her eyebrows. "For me?"

"You don't know for sure if the Bs are thieves, but now you know that I'm one!" He pulled another strawberry pie out of his bag. "Mr. Franko doesn't have zombitus, and yet he still always forgets to lock the home ec room when he leaves."

Megan drooled at the sight of the slightly moldy, oddly colored dessert.

"Dive in," he told her.

And Megan did.

The week passed by in a rush. On Friday night, Megan met Sam in the darkened passageway that ran beneath the tower room.

"You really do know your way around the castle," Megan whispered, impressed that they were in a place they could hear everything going on, but not be seen.

"Sometimes being somewhere a long time has its benefits," Sam replied. He touched Megan's shoulder and pointed out the best spot for eavesdropping.

"How long have you been — ?" Megan began to ask, but voices in the tower room interrupted her.

"Where's Yeverman?" Brenda asked.

Megan closed her eyes to picture the scene. Brenda was undoubtedly wearing one of her many tire-track dresses. The others were less predictable, but Megan imagined whatever Betsy had on was probably spotlessly clean.

"I don't know," Brooke replied. "I told her to be here."

"She told us she'd be *here*," Megan whispered to Sam.

"Who told you what?" Sam asked. "Where's Happy?"

"Exactly," Megan said.

"She's going to help us, right?" Betsy asked.

"For sure she's helping," Brooke said with a bitter chuckle. "She knows that I know who she is. She doesn't want her secret revealed. She'll do what I tell her to do."

Under the tower, Sam gave Megan a sideways look.

"She's Yeverman," Megan revealed, realizing that Sam was completely baffled.

"Happy Yeverman?" Sam had no clue.

Megan couldn't remember Happy's whole name. "It's Henrietta something something," she told Sam. "Yeverman's her last name."

"That makes sense," Sam said softly. "I thought her parents gave her the wrong first name."

"They kind of did." Happy was happier not being a Yeverman. With Happy's permission, she'd explain everything to Sam later. He clearly didn't know anything about the fashion industry.

"As long as she's got the stuff ready by Visitors' Day," Brenda said.

"Oh, she will," Brooke said with another chuckle. "And she'll get a huge surprise when she sees who's in the audience."

"By then it'll be too late," Betsy said. "For everyone!"

The Bs all laughed. Their voices echoed off the stone walls of the tower.

"Okay," Megan whispered to Sam. "We can go. I think I know what's going on."

"What?" Sam still had no clue.

"The cure," Megan told him.

"What about it?"

"Well, they —" Megan began, but then she heard the Bs ending the meeting.

"I love being a zombie." Megan didn't know if Brenda meant *Zom-B*, as in popular, or *zombie*, as in undead. Megan immediately thought about when Zach said that some people may not want to cure zombitus. Could the Bs have stolen the cure to make sure no one got better? What did Brenda mean when she said, "It'll be too late"?

Quickly, she wrote her questions down so she could think about them later.

Megan and Sam sat silently until they were sure the Zom-Bs had left. Then they snuck down the passageway and out into the main hall.

When they reached the koi pond, Brett was waiting, hands on his hips, snarling.

"Aha!" Brett pointed at Megan. "I knew it." The Bs were with him. It appeared as if they'd been waiting for her.

"Knew what?" Megan pretended that she and Sam were just now crossing to the elevator, coming from the . . . she looked around, but couldn't think of a good excuse, so she improvised. "We were walking around the castle." Pause. "What's going on?"

"You were in the tower," Brett accused Megan. His one sharp tooth glinted in the moonlight. "I could smell you."

Megan sniffed her arm. "I don't smell special," she said.

"Liar!" Brett boomed. "My sense of smell has gotten better since I started transforming. You smell like the ocean in Dana Point."

Whew. That wasn't so bad. Megan was worried her deodorant wasn't working or her breath reeked.

"You were there." He poked his finger at Megan and Sam. "Spies!"

Megan hadn't heard Brett at the meeting and now she understood why. Whatever was going on, the Zom-Bs felt that it was important enough to put Brett on guard duty.

"Oh, come on, Brett," Sam said, putting his arm around Megan's shoulder. He gave Megan a little squeeze. "We weren't spying. We're on a date. Everyone knows how much I like Megan. I'm lucky she agreed to hang out with me tonight." Sam pulled Megan closer. "I wanted to show her the full moon." He grinned. "It's so bright tonight."

A zombie's body temperature was normally cooler than a regular person's. Yet as she leaned into Sam, Megan was sure her temperature spiked a couple thousand degrees. She worried that if she got any hotter, her hair would set itself on fire.

Brett looked at Megan for a long time, as if he was remembering something. But the glimmer in his eyes disappeared as fast as it came.

"I don't believe you," he told Sam.

That hurt. Why wouldn't he believe Megan was on a date with Sam? It could happen, couldn't it?

"Uhhhh-uhhhh," Brett groaned and then he leaped forward. "Spies! Get them!" he yelled.

Sam and Megan took off running, with the Ghouls close behind. But they were easy to ditch. Betsy refused to get messy, so she never actually ran after them at all. Brenda was so out of shape she walked more than she ran. Plus, shuffling straight legged in high heels slowed her down. Brooke, it turned out, had asthma. She ended up bent over, leaning on her knees, using an inhaler, and breathing heavily while Sam and Megan got away.

Brett was the only one still chasing them. Megan wondered what he'd do with her and Sam if he caught them. A picture of him eating brains at a long table set with candles and cloth napkins popped into her mind and made her run faster.

"I'll distract him," Sam said, turning away from Megan. "I know all the passageways." He glanced back over his shoulder at Brett. "You'll never catch me, Zom-Bonehead!"

Megan headed toward the back door. Outside, she'd have a better chance to hide until it was safe.

Unfortunately, Brett followed Megan out into the cool night air.

Since they weren't in the same PE class at home, she'd never seen him run, so Megan was surprised when Brett began gaining on her. He was the fastest zombie she'd ever seen! Almost supernaturally fast.

Running was not going to save her.

Brett made a grab for the back of Megan's black T-shirt and she stumbled.

Rocks scraped Megan's hands and knees as she lunged out of Brett's grasp. She managed to stand, but Brett was only inches behind her.

"I've got you!" Brett snarled. "I've been waiting

for this moment ever since you turned me into a zombie!"

"What are you talking about?" Megan kicked and struggled.

"I ate your disease-infected brownie!"

"I can't believe you think I gave you zombitus," Megan said. She still had no idea how she'd gotten it in the first place.

"It was *your* brownie!" he shrieked. His angry face was centimeters from hers.

"Don't blame me! I didn't force you to eat it." She tried every move she'd learned from wrestling with Zach, but Brett was too strong. "Get away from me, you snaggletooth!"

"Now you have to pay," he said quietly.

More scared than she'd ever been her whole life, Megan stopped fighting and closed her eyes. If this was the end, to be eaten alive by her first crush, she didn't want to see it. She hoped it would be quick and painless.

"What's going on here?"

Saved!

Megan knew that voice. She opened her eyes slowly. She also knew those floral flip-flops.

Looking up past Brett's big pumpkin head, Megan was relieved to find Mr. Jones standing over them.

"Mr. Hansen?" Mr. Jones pulled Brett off of Megan with a strong hand. "Is this appropriate zombie behavior?"

Megan scrambled up and ducked behind Mr. Jones's large body for protection.

"I —" Brett began to explain, but Mr. Jones cut him off.

"I will not have my students eating other students," Mr. Jones's said. "This is a vegetarian campus." No one had told Megan that. Sam and Happy had just let her assume brains would eventually be served in the cafeteria.

"I wasn't going to eat her," Brett said, quickly defending himself.

"And what were you planning to do?" Mr. Jones stared hard at Brett.

Yeah . . . Megan wanted to know, too.

"Megan and I are old friends from Dana Point," Brett explained. "We were just playing around." He laughed, but it was obviously forced.

Mr. Jones turned to Megan. "Is that true?"

Brett licked his lips nervously. Whether he meant it as a threat or not, Megan got the chills. She wanted to get away from Brett as soon as she could.

"Um . . . I'm Megan Murry. I'm new here. Can I talk to you about something?" she asked Mr. Jones.

Drawing his bushy eyebrows together and lowering his eyes, he looked between her and Brett and back again.

"Alone," Megan said, nodding her head toward Brett.

When Mr. Jones didn't reply, she added, "It's important."

"If I *ever* catch you chasing one of my students," Mr. Jones said, his European accent crackling, "you will be transferred to my school in Siberia." A small smile curled his mouth. "It's lovely. Old historic property. On Lake Baikal at the base of a mountain." Mr. Jones wrapped his arms around himself and with a shiver, warned Brett, "It's cold in Siberia. Very, very cold."

"Yes, sir." Brett scampered off to the dorms.

"You have something to tell me?" Mr. Jones asked Megan when they were alone. He tapped a flip-flop impatiently. "Something vital?"

"Umm." Megan was grateful for the rescue. But at the same time, the man made her very nervous.

Sam had told her he was nice. She trusted Sam.

Megan took a deep breath. "The Bs stole the zombitus cure."

CHAPTER TEN

Mr. Jones's house looked amazingly similar to Dr. Shelley's office. If they didn't know each other already, they should. When Megan had first come down with zombitus, she'd gone to see Dr. Shelley and been surprised at all the monster-movie stuff that decorated the doctor's office. Mr. Jones had more of the same kind of things. If they ever met, they could trade monster-movie lunch boxes and play make-believe with their zombie figurines.

Of course, mixed in with all his monster collectables, Mr. Jones also had his Hawaiian thing going. Hula-girl bobbleheads danced on a shelf next to werewolf figurines. A small, child-size coffin sat in the corner of the room on top of a grass-woven rug. A black painting (could it be Happy's work?) was hanging inches away from a photo of the sun setting over a beach in Honolulu.

Megan scooted herself back into one of Mr. Jones's overstuffed floral-print chairs. The chairs matched his shirt and Megan couldn't help but wonder what the famous Yeverman parents would think of designing a room to match a wardrobe. Or a wardrobe to match a room, Megan wasn't sure. Might be a new trend. She tried to laugh at the situation, but her nerves were on fire.

Mr. Jones left the room for a minute and when he returned, Megan discovered something important. Yes . . . drinks at ZA were served with mini umbrellas. Her Coke had a pink one stuck in the straw.

Megan sipped her soda for a long quiet moment. Mr. Jones sat down in a comfy chair that faced hers.

"You've made a broad accusation," he said while sipping a Coke of his own. "What brings you to your conclusion?" His accent seemed stronger at night. He sounded an awful lot like what Megan imagined Dracula sounded like.

Megan toyed with her umbrella, trying not to notice that soda was gurgling out the sides of Mr. Jones's mouth, making the bloodstains there turn a muddy brown. She took a deep breath. "Because

I saw . . ." She tapped her chin. "I saw . . . What did I see?"

Blasted zombitus brain fog!

Unable to remember all the details, she opened her red notebook and reviewed her notes.

"The Zom-Bs —" She paused to make certain Mr. Jones knew who she was talking about. When he identified Brooke, Betsy, and Brenda, she went on. "The day after the cure was stolen, I saw the Zom-Bs coming out of the research center," Megan said. "They were carrying a bag of glass tubes. I think they had the vials of the cure."

Mr. Jones was intrigued. "Go on," he told her, wiping his face on a handkerchief.

"They came out a broken window."

"Did you see them break the window?" Mr. Jones asked. He was now taking notes in his own ZA notebook.

"No," Megan said honestly.

"Hmmm. Did the girls say they had taken the cure?" Mr. Jones asked.

"No," Megan admitted. "But they said that after whatever they're planning to do on Visitors' Day, no one will care that the cure was stolen."

"Do you know what they are planning?" Mr. Jones chewed the end of his pencil until it splintered.

"Uhh." This wasn't going so well. "No," Megan said again.

"I see." Mr. Jones tucked his pencil into his notebook and closed the cover. Megan waited to hear what he'd make of her suspicions while he took his time finishing his drink. "Ms. Murry," Mr. Jones said after what felt like an endless silence. "It is not kind to accuse without proof."

"But I do have proof!" She had one more thing to tell him. "They like it here!" Megan blurted, trying to convince him that she was right. "Brooke, Betsy, and Brenda *like* being zombies. They don't want to get cured. They aren't popular at home. They're only cool here. The Bs stole the cure so they can rule the school forever!"

At that, Mr. Jones laughed. Not the normal laugh of an older man, but the cackling chuckle of a witch. Megan shrank back in her chair, hoping that he hadn't saved her from Brett so that he could have her brains all for himself.

"Oh dear, Ms. Murry," Mr. Jones said as his laughter died down. "If that is your criteria for thieving, then you must add me to your suspect list. I, too, love it here. I do not wish to be cured. I have built the perfect home for myself. I also hope to stay a zombie forever." He waved his arm around his bungalow and said, "Have you considered that perhaps I stole the cure?"

Megan got an instant headache. "I thought you were getting the first dose." She didn't understand.

He pointed to the coffin in the corner. "That is not made for a body. It's a locked safe for my most valuable things." He turned to face Megan, his eyes glowing softly as he said, "I want a vial to save for posterity."

Glancing around the room, Megan asked, "To add to your collection?"

Mr. Jones chuckled. "Exactly. One more thing for my *collection*."

He rose and walked Megan to the door. "It's late. Go back to the dorms." Moonlight illuminated the path. "Stop pretending you're a detective," he said. "There is no mystery here. Relax. Don't worry about the cure. Someday my researchers will find one, but today is not that day. In the meantime, I suggest you hang loose. You might find you like it here."

Megan shook her head. "No disrespect, sir, but I *want* to go home."

Mr. Jones squinted at Megan and scratched his chin. "Yes," he said. "I understand. Your friend Sam used to say that, too." He added, "In time, he came to see the advantages of being a zombie. So will you."

With a soft click, Mr. Jones closed the bungalow door behind Megan.

CHAPTER ELEVEN

"He doesn't get it," Megan muttered to herself as she headed back to the castle. She was frustrated. "He doesn't want to be cured."

Megan hurried toward her dorm room. Her knees kept locking, which made running difficult. But she wanted to sit on her bed and write down her conversation with Mr. Jones in her notebook before she forgot.

She was concentrating so hard on not forgetting that Megan didn't see the guy waiting for her by the castle door.

"Megan," he said.

"AUGH!" She jumped and turned to run as fast as her straight legs could go.

"Wait!" the guy cried after her. "It's me."

Megan was having a hard time processing who "me" was. Her brain fog felt foggier than usual. And the moonlight made her vision blurry. Terrified that Brett was back to eat her brains, Megan hurried toward the cottage. Mr. Jones was strange and she didn't trust him, but she had nowhere else to go.

"Megan!" Sam yelled after her. "It's me, Sam."

"Oh." Megan felt foolish for running away. She slowed to a stop and waited for him to catch up. Her heart was beating so hard, she wondered if it would ever settle back to a normal rhythm. They were on the pathway to Mr. Jones's, near the break off to the research center.

"I was worried about you. I've been searching all over for you," Sam said. The way he was squinting at Megan made her uneasy. "You feeling okay?"

"Uh, yeah," she lied. She wasn't feeling okay at all. The combination of what had happened with Brett and the fact that Mr. Jones didn't believe her was making Megan's head feel full. Plus, she had a toothache and her brain felt like oatmeal.

She looked up at the moon. It was full, big and round and reddish. What did Zach call it when it looked like that? *A hunter's moon.* The thought made her shiver.

"I was afraid that Brett —" Sam said, looking at Megan with a frown.

"He almost did," Megan said. He didn't seem like a brain sucker, but then again, Megan had no idea what Brett would have done had Mr. Jones not showed up. "Mr. Jones saved me," she told Sam.

"Told you he was nice." Sam's frown flipped to a grin.

"He still scares me," Megan admitted. "I think Mr. Jones might have stolen the zombitus cure."

Sam laughed. "No way."

Megan told him how Mr. Jones said that she might like it at ZA if she'd give it a chance.

"He's protecting you," Sam said, defending the old man. "Remember how upset you were when you found out there was a cure and then found out there wasn't? It keeps happening. He just wants you to get into the routine of school and stuff."

"I don't know. . . ." Megan's detective mind was spinning.

"I thought you said the Bs took the cure?" Sam asked.

"I did," Megan said. A possibility took form. "Maybe they're all working together."

"You're getting goofy," Sam said. "Mr. Jones didn't tell the Bs to take the cure. He's hired researchers and built a fancy lab. He wouldn't waste his money by finding a cure just to steal it himself."

"Unless . . ." The mystery was becoming clearer. "Unless he has so much money that he doesn't care," Megan retorted. "Did the cure ever go missing before the Bs got here?"

Sam considered the answer. "I'll admit that the Bs have been here every time a cure was stolen." He stopped Megan before she could shout *Aha!* "But the doctors hadn't even discovered a cure until a few years ago."

Megan didn't hear what else he said until Sam put a hand on her shoulder and gave her a little shake. "You're thinking so hard that you're zoning out. Listen to me. It's not Mr. Jones," Sam said.

She didn't believe him. "So, do you think the Bs stole the cure on their own?"

"No," Sam said. "I don't."

"Then what are they up to?" Megan asked. "What was going on in the tower?"

"I don't know," Sam said. "But I'm certain it wasn't about the cure."

"If you're so sure it wasn't the Bs or Mr. Jones, who do you think took it?" When he didn't answer right away, Megan plowed forward. "See! It has to be the Bs or Mr. Jones. There are no other suspects!"

"Uhhhh-uhhhh!" Sam groaned. It was the first time Megan had heard him go full-on zombie. "Can we talk about this later?" He looked around. "Privately?"

Sam was irritated with her and Megan didn't understand why. She was about to solve the mystery. "Why are you arguing with me?" Megan asked him.

"I'm not," Sam said. "I just don't want to discuss this anymore."

"Then why are you arguing with me?" Megan wouldn't let it go. "Mr. Jones obviously convinced the Bs to steal the virus cure." She knew she was right. Why didn't Sam see that she was right?

"I'm not arguing. You're being impossible," Sam replied.

"Mr. Jones didn't believe me about the Bs and now you don't believe me about Mr. Jones."

"You're jumping to conclusions."

"Am not!"

"Are, too!" One of Sam's fingers fell off just then. He quickly scooped it up and stuffed it into his pocket.

"See?" Megan said, feeling like her head was about to burst from being so very right. "Nurse Karen says zombie transformations happen when we get too emotional, so that proves you *are* arguing with me." She pointed at Sam's pocket.

"I guess I am!" Sam gave up. "This conversation doesn't make sense. Why would Mr. Jones use the Bs like that?"

"Because he didn't want to do the dirty work himself," Megan responded, stifling the urge to add Zach's catchphrase: *Duh!*

Sam let out a long sigh. "Can we finish this conversation tomorrow? We aren't getting anywhere. I already lost a finger. And you —" He reached out to touch Megan's hair. "Let's stop fighting. Get some rest. It's been a long day."

She flinched and pulled back. "Don't touch me," she said.

"But there's a —" Sam let his hand drop to his side.

"I know what I'm talking about." Megan's loud voice cut through the night. "Mr. Jones and the Bs are in this together. I have to find the cure and steal it back." She added, "I'm not speaking to you again until you admit that I'm right." Megan turned, and stormed into the castle.

"You're wrong," Sam called out after her. "Dead wrong."

When Megan entered the dorm room, she was surprised to find Happy sketching ideas for a new painting. It was after two in the morning.

"You look rotten," Happy said as Megan closed the door. "Where have you been?"

"Thanks. I feel rotten," Megan replied in a snippy voice. "But I think the question should be: Where have *you* been?"

"Huh? I've been here all night." Happy ruffled the papers she was working on. "Making ugly drawings for a lame project. Why?"

Megan didn't sit. She paced the room, saying, "You were supposed to meet me and Sam at the tower to spy on the Bs." Saying his name made her feel even angrier. She couldn't believe he doubted her!

"I forgot about it." Happy pressed too hard on her black charcoal pencil and snapped off the tip. "Sue me."

Megan said, "Did you forget to meet up with the Bs, too?" The question came out like an accusation.

Happy noticed. "What's wrong with you?"

There was so much emotion boiling inside Megan, she couldn't control it anymore. All Megan wanted was to get cured and go home, but no one was going to help her! In fact, everyone at Zombie Academy was working against her.

"What's wrong with *me*? What's wrong with *you*?" Megan blurted. "The Bs say you're doing something with them on Visitors' Day."

"Yeah. So what?" Happy didn't explain. She was really good at staying calm. No wonder she barely looked like a zombie.

Megan, on the other hand, was seething. "Brooke says if you don't help the Bs with their plan, she'll reveal who your parents are to the whole school!"

"Brooke's a Mean Ghoul." Happy shrugged. "She's mean to you. She's mean to me. You seem surprised."

"Get real. I saw you hanging out with her in science. You were laughing. And you *never* laugh! I think the Bs stole the cure," Megan said. "And I think you know where it is!"

"Oh, come on, Megan," Happy said. "It was home ec, not science. And I wasn't laughing. You're not remembering correctly."

"I —" When pressed, Megan actually couldn't say for sure if Happy had been laughing or not, but it had felt like she was at the time.

"You have zombitus brain," Happy told Megan. "If you stopped and thought about what you were saying, you'd realize —"

"I know the Bs have the cure. And since you're such good friends with Brooke, tell me, Happy, where is it?!" Megan was sure that her brain was working perfectly. "Did they give it to Mr. Jones? Do *you* have it? I need that cure!"

"Go to the nurse, Megan," Happy said calmly. "You're flipping out and it's making your zombie transformation accelerate."

"I am not —" Megan started, but then Happy held up a small hand mirror and turned it toward Megan.

Sure enough, when Happy gave Megan the mirror and she took a long look at herself, she saw that her two front teeth were nail sharp and a stripe of gray had grown into her hair.

That explained why Sam was staring at her so strangely. Then he went and argued with her and made it all worse!

"Zombitus makes everyone a little nutty," Happy explained. "Ask Sam. He once told me that the first time he lost a finger, he freaked out, rode his horse to the pier, and blew out the night lamps. Then, he cut a bunch of ropes, releasing the boats attached to them into Seattle's harbor. It was a disaster. Mr. Jones convinced Taft to let Sam come here instead of going to prison."

"Always the hero, that Mr. Jones, isn't he?" Megan snorted as she stared at herself in the mirror. Okay, so she was going through some small zombitus changes. But that didn't affect what she knew to be true. She faced Happy. "Why won't you tell me where the cure is?"

When Happy refused to answer, Megan's anger peaked into a fireball. She threw the mirror down on the floor. "I thought we were friends!" she shouted.

Happy stared at the shards of mirror that littered the floor. "That's seven years' bad luck," she said. "As if my luck's not bad enough."

Megan couldn't think straight. Both her legs locked super-straight, her arms suddenly shot forward, and she stumbled across the room like a full zombie. "Uhhhh-uhhhh." Flinging her arms around, Megan knocked over Happy's drawings.

They weren't for a painting after all.

And they weren't black either.

Happy scrambled to pick up her sketches, but Megan had seen enough to know that Happy was keeping a huge secret. Happy was designing clothing. Each outfit was drawn in colored fabrics, with gauzy scarves and coordinating shoes and purses. There were fancy prom dresses and casual wear. All of it clean and neat.

"Uhhhh-uhhhh," Megan groaned again. "Tell me where the zombitus cure is!"

"Get out of *my* room," Happy told Megan, her voice strong and yet, still calm. "Go see Nurse Karen. She's an expert in massage, biofeedback, yoga, and acupuncture. And she's on duty 24/7. You have to calm down so that you won't transform anymore."

"This is *my* room, too. I don't have to see the nurse if I don't want to. I don't have to leave if I don't want to."

"Stay, then. It's a free castle." Happy went back to drawing.

"Ugh!" Megan grabbed her pillow and her red ZA notebook. She shuffled to the door. "I'm leaving."

"Whatever." Happy shrugged.

"I'm going to find that cure," she told Happy.

Megan left the room, slamming the door behind her. She shouted her last words through the solid wood. "I can't be friends with a thief!"

CHAPTER TWELVE

Saturday morning, Megan woke up in the school library. She'd fallen asleep while searching the mystery section for a cool young detective who didn't need sidekicks. Certainly, in centuries' worth of literature, there must have been one who wasn't old and stale. At about five A.M., she fell asleep, curled up on her dorm-room pillow with stacks of novels surrounding her like low walls.

She yawned and stretched before sitting up. Blinking against the harsh fluorescent lights, Megan picked up her ZA notebook and reviewed everything that had happened the day before.

She was mad at Sam. She was suspicious of Happy. Mr. Jones wanted her to be a zombie forever, and Brett wanted to eat her brains.

"Another day at Zombie Academy," Megan moaned as she gathered her things and headed to the bathroom to wash her face.

Looking in the mirror was horrifying. Her hair stood straight up as if she'd been electrocuted. No matter how Megan tried, she couldn't get it back down. Even tossing water on her head didn't work. Gravity was working against her, and Megan's auburn curls boinged right back up when they dried.

Her knees were stiff, but she could bend them now. Her sharp teeth were annoying. Then again, Megan could open tin cans if she needed to. And the gray stripe in her hair . . . well, it almost looked like she'd bleached her hair on purpose. Very classy.

Megan didn't need Nurse Karen. She knew what she needed to do, and it wasn't hanging loose or resting or calming down. Megan was focused. She was going to find out where the Bs stashed the cure so she could get home to Dana Point. And she knew exactly how to find it. With the skeleton key Zach gave her, she could search the Bs dorm room!

But she'd have to wait until later that afternoon. Saturday classes started with Zombie History.

Entering the classroom, Megan looked for a place to sit. Sam sat with Happy. The Bs, including Brett, took up the back row. There was an empty desk on one side of the room, next to a girl with long red stringy hair named Reena. She didn't seem to have a nose, just a big boney hole where one used to be. That was the desk Megan chose.

As she sat down, Megan realized immediately why the seat was empty. For some people, the zombitus virus attacked their flesh and decayed their skin, which smelled pretty gross. Like the driver who brought Megan to school. And apparently poor, poor Reena. No one sat by her because she stank.

Since Megan had no other friends, she tried to ignore the stench and be friendly.

"Hi," she said to Reena while glancing over her shoulder at the Bs.

"Uhhhh-uhhhh," Reena groaned at Megan.

"You've got it bad, huh?" Megan said.

Reena nodded.

"I think I can help. I'm going to make sure you get some of the cure when I find it," Megan told Reena.

Class began, but Megan couldn't concentrate. Twice she tried to see if she could hear what the Bs were whispering about and leaned back so far she nearly fell out of her chair.

The third time she heard them whispering, Megan actually did fall out of her chair. She hit the floor with an echoing *bang*.

Brett laughed. Brooke pointed. Brenda tapped her heel. And Betsy said something in Spanish that couldn't have been nice.

"Here, let me help you." Sam came over and offered his hand to help Megan up.

But she couldn't look at him. "I can't be friends with thieves. Or people who don't believe in me. That's how friendship works."

Sam just shook his head and walked away.

Science was equally lonely, and this time when one of the Bs ruined Megan's lab experiment, there was no one there to help her. Happy didn't offer. The gooey purple solution burned a nickel-size hole in the back of Megan's left hand. Dr. Verma put a green gel ointment on it and told her to keep her whole arm elevated for the next three hours.

With one hand raised in the air, Megan got called on repeatedly in home ec.

By the end of Saturday's classes, she was ready to stop worrying about schoolwork and start sleuthing.

Everyone at school was buzzing about the newest

movie showing in the theater. It was a prerelease for Halloween. Even critics hadn't seen it yet. But since Mr. Jones was an adviser to the director, the school got a first look. Showtime was at twelve thirty. Megan didn't want to see another horror movie. She'd seen enough with Zach.

While the Bs were at the film, Megan made her way to the dormitory wing so she could take a look around their room. She stared at the three stars with their names printed on them. The door seemed to twinkle at her.

Megan's heart raced. She'd never actually broken into anywhere before. Then again, she'd never had to. The mixture of guilt for invading the Bs' privacy and the thrill of the hunt for the missing cure made her edgy.

As she used the skeleton key to open the lock, her raging emotions caused a third tooth to sharpen into a spike. If her dentist saw her now, he'd put her in braces for sure. With rubber bands, a retainer, and headgear all at the same time.

The lock clicked and Megan silently thanked her brother for his gift. She opened the door just enough to slip inside.

Very carefully, Megan set her ZA notebook on the

floor by the door. She didn't want to forget anything she saw.

A calendar on the wall had next Sunday's date circled. Visitors' Day. And under that it said in bright red pen, *Destroy.*

"That's it!" Megan said a little too loudly. The Bs were going to destroy the cure on Visitors' Day.

Megan couldn't let that happen. She had to find the vials. Fast.

She opened Brenda's desk drawer and found three pictures tucked under a stack of yellow stationery. The first was a photo of Brenda in the blue prom dress she'd been wearing the first day Megan saw her. Only it wasn't ruined and the tire tracks that stained it were missing. It was actually very pretty. And so was Brenda. In another photo, Brenda sat behind the wheel of a jeep, driving over a stack of dresses. Why would she do that?

Hadn't Happy said that people did weird things when they found out they had zombitus? Megan imagined that Brenda always loved frilly dresses. Then when the disease kicked in, she went loopy, stole her mother's keys, and trashed all of her favorite clothes. Maybe she thought if she was going to become a zombie, she should look like one, too.

The third picture showed Brenda getting into the ZA limousine while her family stood by, waving. Brenda had three sisters. One was a baby.

Megan put the pictures back and took a look at Betsy's desk.

The drawer was empty. There wasn't even one speck of dust.

"Figures," Megan muttered.

She was starting to feel like Goldilocks. *I guess it's down to Baby Bear's desk*, she thought.

Brooke's drawer was locked. The Bs must have stored the vials inside. Megan felt her newest zombie tooth sharpen as her heart raced. Her skeleton key fit perfectly in the lock.

Megan turned the key half a click to the left and the drawer popped open. Inside all she found was a copy of the English class essay on *Frankenstein* and a packet of crushed flowers. Megan smelled the flowers. Lavender and roses and orange blossom.

With a sharp exhale, Megan realized that she hadn't found the answer she wanted. She put the packet back in the drawer, closed it, and relocked it.

She looked under all three beds and in all three closets.

There was nothing out of place and nothing that looked like the glass vials she'd heard clink in Brooke's bag. *Maybe I was wrong about the Bs*, she thought grudgingly.

As Megan headed out the door, she bent down to grab her notebook off the floor, and that's when she saw it. There was a crate next to Brenda's desk. It had a lamp on top, and it looked like a regular nightstand. Except for the big padlock.

She tried to pick the lock with her skeleton key, when Megan heard the Bs' voices outside the window. The movie couldn't be over yet. What were they doing back so soon? There wasn't time to open the crate. She'd just have to take the whole thing and open it later.

Only it was way too heavy. She tried shoving it toward the hall door, but it wouldn't budge. *Uh! I'll just have to come back later.* She put the lamp back the way she'd found it.

Megan heard Brett's "uhhhh-uhhhh" groan getting closer. It sounded like the Bs were down the hall by the bathrooms. There was a mirror in the hallway.

"That movie was so lame," said Brooke.

"No kidding," Brenda agreed. "That's why we left."

"Zombies may live in graves in the movies," said Betsy, "but who'd actually sleep in the dirt? Eww."

Megan had to get out of the room before they caught her. She tiptoed out the door and dashed to her own room next door. She spotted Brett standing by the bathroom door, looking bored while he waited for the Ghouls to finish fixing their lip gloss. Luckily, he was playing on his phone. Megan fumbled with her room key, and just as Brett raised his head toward her, the lock clicked and she slipped inside.

Breathing heavily, Megan leaned against the wall. She'd found the cure! The Bs really had stolen it. It felt good to be right. She'd have to write down what she'd learned so she'd remember to go unlock that crate later.

That's when she remembered something important. She'd brought her red Zombie Academy notebook into the Bs' dorm room.

And she'd left it there.

CHAPTER THIRTEEN

Megan had to get the notebook back. She had no choice. Inside those pages were her notes about the cure and her friends at home and every day she'd been at ZA. It would be embarrassing if that stuff was made public. And she knew the Bs would relish any opportunity to humiliate her. There was no way they'd keep that stuff to themselves. Especially when they discovered she'd been investigating them.

Pushing all her fears aside, Megan dashed back out into the hall.

But she was too late. Brooke was already standing in the doorway of her room holding it. "Whose is this?"

"It's mine." Megan used her fastest soccer kick to

knock the book out of Brooke's hand. It fell back to the floor, where Betsy quickly scooped it up.

Imagining she was going after a ball, Megan stretched her leg forward the way she would for a penalty kick, and using the side of her foot, shoved the notebook hard. It slid under Brenda's bed.

Megan dove for it, but Brenda was closer. "What's your notebook doing in our room?"

"I —" Megan didn't have an excuse. If she accused the Bs right now, they might never let her go. She was in enemy territory. "I dropped it and accidentally kicked it under your door. I've been waiting for you guys to come back so I could get it. Can I have it now?"

"I don't think so," Brenda said. "I'm going to read it."

"Don't!" Megan protested as Brenda opened the notebook.

On the first page, Megan had written a paragraph about meeting Sam. To her horror, Brenda began to read it out loud.

"*'He's cute.'*" Brenda imitated Megan's voice. "*'In a nerdy kind of way.'*" She giggled.

"Noooo!" Using every ounce of energy she had, Megan dove for the notebook again.

Brenda pulled it away at the last second, tossing the notebook across the room to Brooke. Megan was moving too fast to stop herself, and she crashed. Hard. Her head hit the side of Betsy's desk. Blood dripped down her cheek. "Head wounds don't heal," Megan muttered as she closed her eyes against the pain. She needed a minute to get herself together.

"*'I invited Rachel to Visitors' Day,'*" Brooke read.

"I know Rachel," Brett chimed in. "We do . . ." He was struggling to remember. "An after-school activity together."

"*'I told Rachel to come to ZA early on Sunday,'*" Brook recited.

It's like my life is flashing before me, Megan thought. *One page at a time.*

"Hey, look, Brett!" Brooke said suddenly. "Megan glued your old online profile in here."

Megan gasped as Brooke tore the page out of her notebook. "That's mine!" she pleaded. "Give it back."

"Let me see." Brett took the page from Brooke. "I have a sister. A dog." He pinched his lips together. "Yep. That's true. But what's this other baloney-maloney? I act in the theater? My favorite color is brown? I don't remember that stuff."

"And you love pepperoni pizza," Megan added. "At least, you used to."

Brett folded the profile page in half. "It all sounds familiar. But I'm not that guy anymore." He waved the printed paper at Megan and then stuffed it in his pocket. "I'm a B." Brett laughed. "A Zom-B!"

The other Bs laughed with him.

"I want my notebook," Megan said.

"No," said Brooke.

"No way," said Betsy.

"It was in our room," Brenda said. "Finders keepers."

"Give her back the notebook." Happy stood in the open doorway. The movie must have ended. "Now."

"Or what?" Brooke said.

"Or I won't do your project," Happy replied.

Megan looked at Happy, relieved to see her. "I thought . . ."

"I know what you thought. And if you think I'm so weak that these Ghouls can blackmail me, then you better rush down to the nurse and have your brain examined. I told you to do that, right?"

"Yeah. You did."

"Well? Did you?"

"No," Megan admitted.

"You should." Happy then turned to Brooke. "The notebook. Now." She held out one hand.

Roles had been reversed. The changes both Happy and Brooke had made when they came to Zombie Academy no longer applied. In this moment, Happy was the tough, popular girl she'd been in middle school in New York.

"If you want your Visitors' Day surprise" — Happy stared at Brooke — "you'll give her the notebook." When no one moved, Happy said, "You need me. I *know* what you are up to."

"How — ?" Brooke really was scared of Happy. Her pale skin seemed more translucent than ever. "Who told you?"

"It all became clear once my parents informed me they were coming to the castle. I'm smarter than you think." Happy squinted. "Now, are you going to give Megan back her notebook, or should I tell Mr. Franko that I quit? You know I'm only helping you because it got me out of PE. I hate shuffle ball. I can ask Mr. Jones for a different project. . . ."

Glancing at her shoes, Brooke handed Megan the ZA notebook.

"We're done here." Happy rotated and left the room. Without looking at the Bs or Brett, Megan clutched her notebook to her chest and followed Happy into the hall.

"I don't understand," Megan said. "After everything I said to you, you didn't have to help me."

"I know." Happy stared hard into Megan's eyes. "Do you still think I helped them steal the cure?"

The vials were in a crate in the room next door. The Bs had definitely taken them, but Megan wasn't sure who else was involved. Was Mr. Jones? Was Happy? Megan's hesitation was answer enough for Happy.

"That's what I thought." she said. "Have a pleasant night in the library."

CHAPTER FOURTEEN

It was four days before Megan had another chance to sneak into the Bs' room. During that time, she'd kept to herself and twitched with anticipation. She couldn't wait to get the vials. She'd go straight to Nurse Karen, get a shot, and be home two hours later.

Wednesday after classes, Mr. Jones announced that there was going to be an assembly near the koi pond. The students were all going to learn an "Aloha" song to greet their guests on Visitors' Day. It was just the distraction Megan needed.

She caught the first few notes from Mr. Jones's ukulele as she entered the Bs' room. She knew that song from her family trip to Hawaii. There were at least three verses. Megan felt confident that she had plenty of time.

Moving the crate was impossible. It was too heavy. So Megan had brought an empty backpack. It would be easier to simply take all the vials and put them in the pack. She'd seen Brooke carrying them out of the research center and she wasn't hunched over, so the crate must have also stored the notebooks and research details the doctors had compiled.

Megan didn't need the notes. Not now. She'd send someone, the police maybe, to get the notes later. All she wanted was the cure.

Everyone was going to be so proud that she'd solved the mystery. She was going to be a hero. It felt good to be right. She couldn't wait to tell Sam.

Just as she'd done before, Megan used her skeleton key to enter the room. She went straight to the crate. And . . .

It was gone.

Where the crate had once stood, a normal table now sat.

For a long minute, Megan wondered if she'd imagined the whole thing. She'd been having so many new zombitus symptoms lately, her mind might be playing tricks on her. Then again . . . the utter humiliation of having her notebook read aloud had felt all too real.

As Megan backed into the hall, her spirits dropped. She was back at the beginning of an unsolved mystery.

The night before Visitors' Day, Megan had a dream.

She was inside Mr. Jones's bungalow, searching for the cure. Ever since the Bs' room turned up empty, she'd been thinking that Mr. Jones might have come to claim the crate.

So there she was, tiptoeing up to the coffin in the corner, when suddenly, Mr. Jones popped out.

Megan screamed.

"I saved you," Mr. Jones said as he climbed out. Even though the coffin was child-size, he seemed to fit just fine. Blood dripped down his chin from sharp-fanged teeth. "I saved you, and still . . . you suspect me."

He reached out and grabbed Megan's hand. She struggled, but he wouldn't let go. His hand tightened around her wrist like a clamp. He circled around her, and Megan felt her heart begin to race. "When Brett was chasing you, I was the one who made him leave you alone. I am the one who makes sure you are safe."

Megan's feet dragged along the carpet as her legs stiffened.

She couldn't bend.

"Uhhhh-uhhhh." She couldn't speak either. Her voice was stuck in a long groan.

"You have turned your back on your friends," Mr. Jones told her. As he loomed over her, she backed closer and closer to the small black coffin.

"Uhhhh-uhhhh." Megan was scared.

Mr. Jones ripped the skeleton key from around Megan's neck.

"Handy little toy. It opens all locks," he said. "Bolts them shut, too."

"Uhhhh-uhhhh!" Megan called for help.

"They won't come," he told her. "They've saved you before. They won't save you again."

Megan didn't have zombie fog head. Her memories were crystal clear.

Sam had pretended to be her boyfriend to get her away from Brett and the Bs outside the castle tower. He'd even tried to get Brett to chase him instead of her.

And Happy had no reason to step in to get Megan's private notebook back from the Bs. But she'd done it just the same.

"No one will save you this time," Mr. Jones repeated as he shoved Megan backward. She struggled against him, but her feet slid across the bamboo rug. "You are alone."

"Uhhhh-uhhhh," Megan groaned.

Inches from the coffin, Mr. Jones scooped Megan up like a child in his arms and dumped her into the box.

"No one will believe you. No matter what you say." He slammed the lid and then used Megan's own key to lock her in. "You are alone," he repeated.

Alone. The word echoed through the blackness. She could smell the stink of her own flesh decaying. Megan gasped for fresh air.

"Alone." Happy's voice reverberated in her ears.

"Alone," said Sam.

"Alone," said Zach.

"Alone," said Rachel.

"Alone," said Brett.

"Alone," said the Bs.

"Uhhhh-uhhhh," Megan cried out. She tried to

raise her arms but they were pinned to her sides. Her legs were stuck straight. Her breath felt hot and shallow. The bottom of the coffin opened and the next thing Megan knew, she was falling into an endless darkness.

With a start, she woke up. And she realized something very important. If she didn't find the cure, she'd be alone forever.

CHAPTER FIFTEEN

On Sunday morning, Megan met her family on the front steps of the school. They wore masks with monster faces painted on them, thanks to Zach.

Megan rushed to give them all a hug. She was even happy to see Zach.

For this special occasion, Mr. Jones had ordered school uniforms. The girls were required to wear a dark pink skirt with a white blouse. The boys had on dark pants with their dress shirts, and pink, plaid ties that matched. Megan pulled back her hair, hoping that her parent's wouldn't notice the zombitus gray streaks.

Her parent's noticed. The first thing Mrs. Murry did was reach out and touch a thick, discolored strand of Megan's hair with her hand. The required plastic glove felt cold against Megan's skin.

"What happened?" her father asked, leaning past Mrs. Murry to examine the gash on Megan's head. "Are you okay?"

"I'm fine," she replied. "Don't worry."

"All part of zombie transformation," Zach told their dad, as if head wounds were to be expected.

Mr. Murry didn't seem to believe Zach, so Zach explained about how getting emotional sped the transformation.

"Grrr." Megan flashed her sharp teeth at him and snarled. "You didn't warn me to stay calm."

"Not my job." Zach shrugged. "Didn't the nurse tell you? She should have."

"Oh, all right," Megan said. "She did. I didn't listen."

"You wouldn't have listened if I said it either," Zach told Megan with a laugh. He was wearing a new T-shirt that said MY SISTER'S A ZOMBIE.

"Nice," Megan told Zach.

"Made it myself," Zach said with pride. "And the masks, too."

"I think you should show —" Megan started to say he should show Happy his fashion creations, but then changed her mind. Happy wasn't her friend anymore.

"Oh, there they are. Dr. Shelley gave Rachel a lift," Mrs. Murry said as a small sedan drove up to the gate. Rachel hopped out while Dr. Shelley went to park.

"Hi, you!" Rachel said, rushing up to Megan.

The two girls hugged for a long time. Megan felt like crying. She knew she'd missed her best friend, but until that moment, she hadn't realized how much.

"I have so many things to —" Megan started, when Rachel suddenly pulled back.

"Hang on one little second," she told Megan as she rushed to where Brett's family was getting out of their own car a few feet away.

"Brett!" Rachel shouted. "The play's not the same without you!"

"Hey . . ." It took him a second to come up with the name. "Rachel." His eyes lit up and Brett gave Rachel a high five, then tugged her in for a hug.

Megan squinted at them. There was something about the way Brett was holding Rachel. Like he wasn't going to let her go. He glanced over Rachel's shoulder and gave Megan a wink.

Brett's sister, Hailey, got out of the family car and looked over at Megan with disgust. Megan was pretty sure that the outfit Hailey was wearing was a Yeverman original. So much for no one knowing that Happy attended the school. Brett must have told Hailey, who immediately went shopping. The dress was way too showy for Visitors' Day and clashed with her white plastic protective gloves and sterile green mask.

The Bs brought their own families over to meet Brett. Hailey and Brenda seemed to hit it off immediately. Brenda looked strange and awkward in her uniform, but soon they were checking out each other's clothing and giggling like best friends. Hailey even picked up Brenda's littlest sister, who was about three years old, and swung her around playfully.

"Hey, Megan." Rachel rushed back to Megan's side. "Brett's new friends asked if I can help them out with a project. It sounds really cool and I'd really like to do it." She was talking very fast. "Would you mind, Megan? I promise I'll make up every minute to you later."

It was one of those questions that was impossible to answer truthfully. Of course she minded. Megan didn't want Rachel to go anywhere with the

Bs. But the way Rachel was looking at her, grinning and excitedly bouncing on her toes — how was Megan supposed to tell her not to go?

"It's fine," Megan said flatly.

"Thanks." Rachel blew a kiss as she rushed back toward Brett and the Bs. "See ya in a while."

Best friends ... Megan's heart felt heavy as Rachel was swept into the Bs' circle and disappeared from sight.

"Come on, Megs." Zach tugged at Megan's arm, bringing her attention back to her own family. "Show us around. I can't wait to meet Mr. Jones. I am sooooo excited."

"Don't get too emotional," Megan warned Zach with a small chuckle. "Or you'll start to transform, too."

"I only wish," Zach said with a pout.

As they entered the castle, Megan's parents were thrilled to see the Hawaiian-themed interior design. They stepped aside to get a better look at a painting of a volcano.

"Your hair and teeth are transformation," Zach whispered to Megan. "But the gash is an injury. I wasn't going to tell Dad that. He'd freak. So, what happened?"

"Long story," Megan said.

"You better tell me," Zach prodded. He put on a monsterish accent and said, "I have vays uff making you talk."

"Don't be such a dork," Megan said, putting him off. "Oh, wait, you can't help it."

Zach gave Megan a playful punch in the arm. She laughed. It was nice knowing that her brother understood about zombitus and zombie life. Still, Megan had decided not to tell Zach about the missing cure and her plans to get it back. He may have been smart, but he was still a little kid.

Dr. Shelley entered the castle on Mr. Jones's arm.

"Look who I found outside," she said after she'd introduced the head zombie to Zach.

Megan hadn't talked to Mr. Jones since the night she'd visited his bungalow. She'd been afraid of him then and the dream she'd had last night had made it worse.

As Mr. Jones stepped toward her, Megan inched back.

Mr. Jones didn't seem to notice. "Nice to meet you, Zach," he said. "I hear you're planning to film scenes for a zombie movie while you're here today."

Zach took a small video camera out of his jeans pocket. "Handheld fright films are all the rage."

"Classic," Mr. Jones said. "I must greet our other guests, but I hope you and Dr. Shelley will join me later for drinks in my bungalow." He turned to Megan. "Please come along. I wouldn't want you to be all *alone*."

Megan gasped. There was no way! He couldn't have known! Dreams were private, weren't they? She wrapped her arms around herself and shivered.

Mr. Jones invited her parents to the gathering and then Megan took them all on a tour of the castle. All except Dr. Shelley. Mr. Jones offered to take her to the research center instead.

"Where's your room?" Zach asked.

"Do you always have to make things so difficult?" Megan replied with a snort.

"Huh?" Zach asked. "What did I say?"

Megan didn't feel like explaining why she'd been living in the library, so she decided the easiest thing would be to take her family to the dormitory to see her room. She hoped Happy wasn't there.

When they got there, Rachel was standing in the dorm hallway with Brett and the Bs. They were looking at the stars on the Bs' door.

"Why don't you have a star on your door?" Rachel asked Megan as she approached.

"I like mine plain," Megan answered.

The Bs laughed and pulled Rachel into their room.

"I'll come next door in a sec," Rachel called out to Megan as she disappeared from the hallway.

Megan groaned. She knew that Rachel would never come by. It wasn't worth waiting. The Bs' power was magnetic. With a deep breath, Megan pretended it didn't bother her, when it really did. It was a struggle, but she managed to keep calm.

"Here it is," Megan said, giving her parents the fastest dorm-room tour in ZA history.

Her side of the room was incredibly neat since she hadn't been there for a week.

Zach took out his video camera and took some footage. "This is going to be the best zombie movie ever. A real zombie's bedroom!"

"Come on, dork. Let's go." Megan grabbed a sweater. "The welcome assembly is starting in a few minutes."

As they were all leaving, Happy and her parents were coming into the room.

Megan closed her eyes and sighed. The last time

Happy had spoken to her was in her dream. And that wasn't real.

"Hey," Megan said, breaking the silence first.

"Hey." Happy's voice was the same, but the Happy who was standing with her parents was not the same Happy that Megan knew. It was the Happy that Megan had seen when she got the notebook back from Brooke. This was New York City's Henrietta Yeverman.

She was wearing a green T-shirt with a long brown skirt. She had gold chains around her neck and a small printed shrug.

"My parents brought me pieces of their new line." Happy gave Megan a threatening look that said, *Don't you dare laugh.*

"Fashion Week was a huge success," Mrs. Yeverman told Megan's mother.

Mrs. Murry hadn't known that Megan's roommate had famous parents. "Tell me more," Mrs. Murry prodded.

An intercom announcement interrupted the dorm-room bonding.

"Everyone, please gather in Room 601." That was the big classroom for Zombie History. "That's 601," the announcer repeated over and over again.

Megan's dad asked, "Why does she keep doing that? 601. Got it. We know where to go."

"Some people have a memory problem because of the zombitus," Megan said, trying to sound like she wasn't one of *those* people.

Room 601 was packed with students and their parents. There wasn't much space inside because a long black catwalk jutted down the center of the room. A curtain covered the back of the catwalk and stage lights cast a golden glow on everything. It was standing room only, which was fine because half the people in the room couldn't bend their legs to sit properly, anyway.

Megan didn't see Rachel. She was probably with Brett, Hailey, and the Bs. . . . Megan told herself not to feel sad. The last thing she needed was another sharp tooth or another gray streak.

Megan glanced around. The little boy who had hugged her in the hallway stood with his parents at the back of the room. Reena and her mother stood by the open window.

Where was Sam? After surveying the entire room, Megan was certain he wasn't there. She opened her notebook to refresh her memory. He'd said no one was around to visit him. But why? She couldn't remember if he'd explained, but if he had, she hadn't written it down.

Dr. Shelley stood to the side of the stage with Mr. Jones. She waved at Megan as the Murrys found a place to stand near the side of the catwalk, where they could see the whole show. And then, the music for the student "Aloha" song began.

Since the moment she'd met her family outside the castle, Megan had acted super mellow, pretending everything was fine. She'd let Rachel run off with the Bs without saying a word about how mean the Ghouls really were. Megan had given her family a tour of the school and acted as if nothing was up between her and Happy. She'd let her family think everything was perfect at Zombie Academy.

Now she was trembling because she knew what the Bs had planned.

In a few minutes' time, they were going to get up on this very stage and destroy the zombitus cure.

But Megan Murry was going to stop them!

CHAPTER SIXTEEN

When the "Aloha" song ended, Mr. Jones got up onstage. The spotlight hit him in the belly, making him look bigger than ever.

"We have a special presentation for you all this afternoon," Mr. Jones said. He'd cleaned the bloody ooze from the sides of his mouth. Megan was glad — she didn't want her parents to be frightened. The whole zombie-school thing was hard enough to deal with. She glanced up at them. They were actually handling everything very well.

"Today, some of our students have prepared something very special for you." He looked directly past Megan to set his eyes on the Yevermans. "I am proud to introduce to you the world of the Zom-Bs:

Brenda, Betsy, and Brooke, along with their designer, Henrietta Yeverman!"

The crowd went wild. Shrieks of "Uhhhh-uhhhh" filled the room along with the traditional "Woo-hoo" from the non-zombies.

Zach was filming everything. He had his camera glued to his eye.

Megan had known there'd be a time when she'd have to sneak away. And this was it.

When the lights dimmed, Megan made her move. She pressed through the crowd closer to the front of the stage.

She'd been exercising in the library every night, getting in shape. Staying calm and keeping her legs limber were the most important things Megan could do to prepare for this moment. After a few knee bends and a few deep breaths, Megan felt ready.

Brenda carried out a small podium and stood behind it. She'd changed into a gauzy fuchsia and green prom dress. Her neck scarf was orange and there were yellow bows in her hair.

"Being a zombie is a way of life," Brenda read from a prepared note card. "Not only for those of us here at Zombie Academy, but soon, for everyone. Everywhere!"

Ha! That's what Megan thought. The Bs were going to make sure everyone stayed at ZA! It sounded like they were going to try to turn other people into zombies, too. Megan's eyes scanned the stage. "The cure has to be here," she muttered. "Where is that crate?"

"Announcing the Zom-B collection." Brenda reached over with one hand and pulled a cord.

The curtain at the back of the stage parted to reveal Rachel, walking down the catwalk like a model, with one hand on her hip. Rachel wore a prom dress like Brenda's, but cuter. It was lilac with a sky blue bow at the waist. Her shoes had matching purple bows above the same-colored blue buckles.

When she reached the end of the stage, Rachel blew a kiss at Megan and mouthed the word *Surprise!* She waved and then rotated on her heel, and turned back down the catwalk.

Next out was Brooke. She was wearing a tight white mummy-gauze dress. There were rhinestones glued all over the gown. It sparkled in the spotlight. Brooke had clearly used spray-on tan, which made her skin look a little less see-through.

Betsy came out arm in arm with Brett. They were wearing casual school clothes. Megan had to admit that Brett looked good in a black T-shirt and jeans. His shirt said BE A B in bold red letters across the front.

Betsy was wearing the same shirt with lace leggings.

At the end of the fashion show, Brenda announced that Happy had helped them with the clothing. Happy came out for a bow, but she didn't look happy.

She took the microphone from Brenda and said, "Hey, Mr. Franko." She squinted into the crowd. "Wherever you are — I did what you asked. I better get an A."

Everyone laughed, though Happy clearly didn't mean it as a joke.

The kids thought the clothing was terrific, but the experts, well, they weren't wowed by their daughter's first fashion show. Mr. Yeverman was checking his e-mail, and Mrs. Yeverman was yawning. Megan could only imagine the pressure they were going to put on Happy to do better next time.

It was beginning to feel like Megan had been wrong all along. Could it have been that the Bs were not planning to destroy the cure, they'd only been planning a fashion show?

Megan was confused. Her detective skills were strong. She knew what the clues meant. Plus, she'd seen that locked crate. She knew they had it. Why had they written *Destroy* on the calendar otherwise?

So many unanswered questions. Her head was beginning to hurt. She wanted that cure!

And then, the lights went out again.

"We have one last surprise!" Brenda announced. "Destroy!"

The curtain flew back and Hailey Hansen came out onto the stage. She was smiling and pushing a cart with the crate on top.

THE CRATE!!

Dressed like a magician's apprentice in a flowing gown, Hailey held up a key, ready to pop the padlock and perform the Bs' most fantastic trick. The one, Megan was certain, that would ensure they all stayed zombies forever.

Hailey bent to unlock the lid, and that's when Megan leaped into action.

Just as the top slid open, Megan threw herself up and onto the stage.

"NOOOOO!" Megan shoved Hailey out of the way. Her middle-school classmate stumbled on a spiked heel and fell off the stage into the crowd.

Brenda, Brooke, and Betsy came rushing after Megan, but she was determined. Using every soccer move she knew, Megan kicked, swung, and head butted them away.

Reaching into the crate, Megan knew she'd find the vials from the research center. And she was right.

Megan grabbed a handful of the small glass tubes and rushed to the side of the stage. "It's the zombitus cure," she told the one person in the room who she knew she could trust. "Don't let the Mean Ghouls get it back!" She gave Zach the vials and rushed back for another load.

Brett was on the stage now with Rachel and Mr. Jones. Even Dr. Shelley was trying to stop Megan.

"Uhhhh-uhhhh!" Megan groaned at them as she stormed past them toward the crate.

"I won't let you destroy the cure!" Megan shouted. She could feel all her remaining normal teeth sharpening at once. Her hair was bleaching itself white. The cut in her forehead burned.

Whirling and grunting and grabbing at anything she could, Megan tried to make a run for more of the vials, but Brenda and Betsy blocked her way. "Uhhhh!" Megan screamed into Brenda's face. Her flailing arms ripped Brenda's Zom-B prom dress until it was a wreck like all her other gowns. Megan shoved Brenda to the edge of the stage. When she was about to fall, Brenda grabbed Brooke to stop herself. Brooke's gauzy dress tore like paper and they both tumbled over the edge onto Hailey, who was squashed beneath them.

"Uhhhh-uhhhh." Megan dodged past Mr. Jones and slammed into Brett. The crate was behind Brett and when he fell backward, the box tipped over. Vials rolled across the stage. Megan flopped to the floor. She wanted to save all the little glass tubes, but there were too many.

Tons of them crashed off the stage and hit the ground with a *splat*. The ones that didn't break right away were getting crushed as visitors and zombie students stepped on them in an attempt to get out of the way.

With each vial that broke open, a scent began to fill the room.

Lavender and roses and orange blossoms.

Why was that smell so familiar?

Megan wished she had her notebook, but she'd dropped it when she first landed on the stage. She could see the red cover near the podium, but it was too far to reach.

Taking as many cure vials as she could carry, Megan made a break for the exit. Once she escaped the castle, she'd go straight to the nearest hospital and ask to be injected. Then, she'd go to the police to explain the mystery and how she'd solved it.

Everyone would be proud. She'd be on the nightly news. A hero.

Suddenly, two strong hands snagged Megan around the waist and pulled her through the curtain, out of sight from the confusion. Megan struggled against her captor, but she couldn't escape. Flopping like a fish, she tried to see who held her. It wasn't Mr. Jones or the Bs or Brett or her family. She knew they were still out there. She could hear them shouting.

The arms held her tighter and a voice said, "Megan, it's me."

"Sam?" Megan stopped fighting for freedom and turned around in his arms. "I'm so glad you're here!" She hugged him tight and then apologized. "Sam, I'm sorry I haven't talked to you all week. But I was right. The Bs took the cure. They were going to destroy it here onstage." Her words were coming out race-car fast. "Please. Help me get the vials. Help me escape." She said the next part in a whisper. "I want to go home."

"I know," Sam said, releasing her. "You have to calm down."

"I can't," she said. "I have to get as many vials as I can so the nurse can save the students." She grinned at him. "We can all go home."

Sam reached out and lightly touched her arm. "The Bs aren't destroying the cure. *Destroy* is the name of the Zom-Bs' new perfume. To go with their fashion line."

"No." She didn't believe him. But as his words sunk in, the scent of perfume filled the room. Even without her notebook, Megan suddenly remembered where she'd smelled it before. The package of flowers in Brooke's drawer. "Oh," she said.

Megan had one last thought before Mr. Jones and the Bs burst through the fashion-show curtain. *I am in so much trouble.*

CHAPTER SEVENTEEN

Megan sat in the same chair in Mr. Jones's bungalow she'd sat in the night she'd solved the Missing Cure Mystery. Which she now knew, she hadn't solved at all.

Her parents were in the next room with Mr. Jones and Dr. Shelley, discussing what to do about the situation.

Megan knew she'd be punished. She assumed she'd be sent away, maybe to the Zombie Academy in Siberia. She'd need a heavier coat.

This was the end. She'd never see her parents again. Or Rachel. Or Dana Point Middle School. She'd never play soccer again either, and with her legs stuck straight, she'd be one of those kids in shuffle ball who ended up falling down a hole all the time.

Megan was going to be a zombie forever. It wasn't even worth looking in the mirror. She'd bitten her tongue enough times to know what had happened to her out there onstage. She was one step closer to full transformation. It wouldn't be long before she craved brains.

Zach could make a movie all about her. . . .

"Hey, sis." Just as she was thinking about him, Zach walked into the room.

"How'd you get in here?" Megan asked, glad to see someone who didn't hate her.

When Mr. Jones took her out of Room 601, the Bs had made it clear how they felt. Brett snarled at her; his one fang had turned into two. Hailey pointed and laughed. Totally embarrassed, Rachel stared at her shoes.

The only one who wasn't mad was Happy.

"You go, girl," she cheered as Megan was escorted away. "That was hysterical!" Happy clapped and then started to laugh. Really laugh. As in holding her belly, falling to the floor, eyes watering laughter.

Megan didn't have time to talk, but she was pretty sure she and Happy would be friends again.

She hoped Happy would send her postcards in Siberia.

Zach sat in Mr. Jones's chair. The seat was so big, his feet didn't touch the floor.

"You've been away a few weeks," Zach told Megan. "You've changed." He pointed to her zombie hair and teeth. "But Mom and Dad are still the same."

"Great parents, terrible hall guards?" Megan said with a small smile.

"Exactly." Zach swung his feet. "Here." He tossed her notebook to her. "I grabbed it before anyone else could."

"Thanks," Megan said, holding her memories on her lap.

"I read the whole thing," Zach admitted.

"What?!" This was as bad as the time he'd read her diary. "You little —"

"You missed some clues," Zach told her. "You almost had the answer, but then . . . you got distracted."

"Obviously," she said. "I destroyed *Destroy* and now I'm going to be a zombie forever." Then, realizing what he meant, she asked, "Wait. You think you might know where the cure is?"

"Yes." Zach nodded. "And who took it, too."

"Don't just sit there. Tell me." If Zach had solved

the mystery, she'd be a lot less mad that he'd read her journal.

"You already know." Zach pointed at the notebook.

"I don't," Megan started to argue. But then, she took a big breath and calmed herself down. There was no point in letting Zach make her zombie symptoms any worse. She wouldn't give him the honor.

Instead, Megan opened her notebook. Slowly, she read each page, looking for clues. If the Bs and Mr. Jones and Happy didn't take the cure, who was left? And what reason did they have to take it?

"Zach," she said at last. "It's so obvious! I can't believe I missed the biggest clues of all."

"You've got zombitus," Zach said with a grin.

"Oh yeah," Megan said, slapping her forehead as if that was another thing she'd forgotten.

Zach laughed.

Megan said, "I know who the thief is, but to get out of here unnoticed, I'm going to need your help."

"I don't think so," he said. "I've already helped you plenty."

"Please," Megan said.

"Oh, fine." Zach made a deal. "I'll distract the adults and help you sneak away. But only if you agree to make a zombie scene for my movie before you get cured."

Megan reached out and shook his hand. "Deal."

"Oh no!" Zach suddenly screamed, as he turned and burst into the room where the Murrys were meeting with Mr. Jones and Dr. Shelley. "I've lost my video camera. We have to search the castle!"

Megan found Sam in the passage under the tower.

"I knew you'd come sooner or later," he said.

Megan sat down. "I'll always remember my first date," she said with a smile.

"It was nice, wasn't it?" Sam smiled for a second. When it faded, he said, "So you figured it out."

"Yeah." Megan opened her notebook. "Zach knew first, but he wouldn't tell me. He made me reread my notebook and solve it for myself."

"That's what makes him an evil genius," Sam said, and Megan laughed.

"I think I understand why you took the cure," Megan told Sam. "You don't want to be alone, right?" Sam nodded.

Just like in her dream. Megan was afraid of being alone, too.

"How old are you?" she asked Sam.

"I was born in 1886."

"I should've known. You said no one comes to Visitors' Day — that's because they're all dead. Happy told me that when you started to become a zombie you blew out lamps — no electricity, eh? And you said you were one of the first students here — Mr. Jones started the school in 1908."

Sam sighed at the memory. "Mr. Jones found me. He got me out of jail and brought me here."

"Oh, right. I forgot, Taft let you come." Megan shook her head. "Another clue that I missed. It took me until today to figure out that 'Taft' meant President William Taft."

"Friendly man," Sam said. "Scared of zombies, though. He was glad to get me out of Seattle and let Mr. Jones be my guardian."

"It must have been hard," Megan said, imagining those first years.

"It was awful. My parents didn't get to say good-bye. They came every Visitors' Day until they were too old to travel. My friends all grew up and had kids and they stopped coming, too. When I got zombitus, I was twelve," he said. "I'm still twelve." Sam told Megan, "The first time the doctors discovered a cure, I stole it. I'd been here so long already, I was worried that everyone would leave." He shook his head. "What would I do? If they ever close the school, I won't have anywhere to go."

"Mr. Jones wouldn't let that happen." Megan was pleased to defend Mr. Jones. Turned out, he was a nice guy after all. He wouldn't let Sam be alone.

Sam shrugged. "It's better for me to stay here. I like it. I have friends. Then you came along and I didn't want you to get cured and leave either."

"I don't belong here," Megan told Sam. "I never did."

"I think today you proved just how much you want to leave." Sam couldn't hold back a brittle laugh.

Megan grimaced. "I added excitement to the welcome show, didn't I?"

"Better than any zombie movie I've ever seen."

"Ha! It will be a zombie movie," Megan said. "Zach filmed the whole thing."

Sam laughed again, but this time he actually seemed pleased. When his giggling faded, Sam reached into his back pocket and handed Megan a vial. "Here's the cure."

She wrapped her fingers around the small glass

tube. It felt like she was holding a magical elixir. In that tube was everything she'd wanted since she first came down with zombitus.

"I wish I'd told you the truth before things got so crazy," Sam said.

Megan flipped open her notebook. "It says right here that you tried. I was already convinced the Bs took it. Nothing you told me would have changed my mind." She tilted her head and smiled at him. "I'm stubborn."

"Yes, you are," Sam said. "I'll explain what happened to Mr. Jones and give him the researchers' notes. Hopefully, he won't punish you too badly."

Megan stood up. "I was looking forward to Siberia," she joked.

"Maybe you can come visit me there," Sam said very seriously.

"We'll always be friends," Megan told Sam. "Wherever you are, I'll visit."

"Promise?" Sam took her hand.

Megan smiled. "Promise."

CHAPTER EIGHTEEN

"I can't believe I'm doing this." Rachel shook her head in disbelief. "I mean, I like acting, but this is —"

"You owe me," Megan said as she climbed into the shallow grave and laid down in the dirt.

"I said I was sorry." Standing nearby, leaning against a tree, Rachel straightened the dress she'd borrowed. It was one of Brenda's favorites, the first one she'd rolled over with the car after she was diagnosed.

"And after this, you'll be forgiven," Megan assured Rachel. "I mean, other best friends might be mad that you came to school and didn't talk to them at all, but not me. I'm totally over the fact that you ran off with the Mean Ghouls."

"I wanted to be part of the fashion show," Rachel explained for the zillionth time. "I thought you'd be surprised. Brett asked me to do it."

"Talking about me?" Brett popped his head out from the open grave next to Megan.

"Yes," Rachel said. "Megan's still mad at us."

"I'm not mad," Megan said. "I know not to get too emotional." She smiled, flashing her sharp teeth. "I still kind of wish you'd have been honest a long time earlier, but seriously, I'm glad that you two are going out." The news hadn't been a surprise. And truly, Megan was fine with it. Brett and Rachel made a cute couple.

Megan rolled on her side to look at Brett. "I forgive you, too, even though you tried to eat my brains."

"You gave me a virus that turned me into a monster!"

"Did not." This time instead of fighting, Megan shrugged and smiled. "At least not on purpose."

"Yeah. I know." Brett sighed. "I just wish someone had given me a zombie rule book. No one told me that there was an unwritten zombie code that zombies don't ever eat other zombies."

In the hours after the fashion-show disaster, Brett

had snapped out of his nastiness. Nurse Karen explained that the shock he'd been in when he'd first arrived had only seemed to disappear, but didn't go away altogether.

"I wasn't in control. I'm not usually mean like that," Brett said. "I had zombitus, you know."

"We both *still* have zombitus," Megan reminded Brett.

They hadn't taken the cure yet because Megan had made a deal. And she'd convinced Brett and Rachel to help her out. They were all going to be in Zach's horror movie.

Brett's and Megan's transformation back to the living was going to be the movie's big climactic scene. But first, Zach wanted a zombie chase.

"Is everyone ready?" Zach asked. He straightened his floppy beret and pointed the video camera at the two graves Dr. Shelley and Mr. Jones had helped dig them in the wooded area near the research center. Happy had painted prop gravestones, and the whole time, she'd complained about working with gray paint, instead of black.

When Megan had returned to Mr. Jones's bungalow with Sam and the cure, there had been a lot to explain. And a lot to apologize for. Turned out, though, that no one was quite as angry as Megan would have expected.

In fact, Rachel and Brett were the first to apologize *to her.* Followed by the Bs.

The Bs had sneakily invited Happy's parents to the show, hoping they'd like the fashion line, but until clothes were thrashed and the perfume spilled, the Yevermans were not interested. After the show, Mr. Yeverman offered to make the torn and fragrant Zom-B chic clothing a part of their fall Halloween-inspired collection

Brenda, Betsy, and Brooke were all going back to their old schools, but thanks to Megan, they'd never be the unpopular girls they were before. They were going to be fashionistas. Megan hoped they'd treat other students better — now that they knew both sides of popularity.

And since the Bs liked fashion and Happy didn't, Happy was also grateful to Megan for getting her parents off her back. They even agreed to let her go to a visual arts high school in a few years.

"Action!" Zach called.

"Augh!!!" Rachel screamed. "Help me!" She dashed through the bushes, looking over her shoulder.

All those years doing theater had made Rachel an excellent actress. Her screams scared Megan so much that for a moment, she forgot that she was supposed to be the scary one!

"Uhhhh-uhhhh," Megan groaned, rising slowly from the grave, tossing dirt aside like Zach had directed.

"Uhhhh-uhhhh." Brett sat up and shook his straight arms.

"Zombies!" Rachel shrieked. She rushed down the narrow path leading to Mr. Jones's cottage.

Megan and Brett kicked off the last bits of dirt and chased Rachel into Mr. Jones's home. Rachel slammed the door. Zach got some great footage of her cowering in a closet while the two zombies stared through the window.

"Cut!" Zach said. He grinned, pleased at how his film was shaping up. Zach went to get Nurse Karen to prepare for the transformation scene. He wouldn't tell Megan what was going to happen. He just kept saying, "This is going to be super-fun!"

While Rachel and Brett congratulated themselves on a job well done, Megan wandered into the living room where Mr. Jones was sitting with Dr. Shelley and Sam.

After confessing to Megan, Sam had come to the bungalow to tell Mr. Jones everything. How he'd taken the cure. And why. He gave back all the researchers' notes and every vial he had stashed in the back of his closet.

The first thing Mr. Jones did was put a vial in his coffin and lock the lid. Now, they sat in his Hawaiian chairs discussing the future. Mr. Jones turned to Dr. Shelley. "Should I ask him?"

She nodded.

Megan couldn't believe what happened next. Mr. Jones and Dr. Shelley announced that they were going to continue to run Zombie Academy for anyone who didn't want to take the cure. But since the school would be much smaller, they'd only need part of the castle. In the other part, they were going to open a haunted hotel.

Dr. Shelley was going to retire from her medical practice and build her own bungalow. She wanted to lead classes on monsters and monster movies. She'd also research zombie health and the benefits of a rotten vegetarian diet. They were going to combine their collectibles and open a museum.

"People will pay big money to visit a zombie haunt," Mr. Jones explained.

"And who better to do it?" Dr. Shelley asked. "I am Mary Shelley's great-great-great-granddaughter after all."

"And I am the son of Mary Shelley's housekeeper, Louisa Jones."

Megan wanted to ask them about her English assignment. *Was Mary Shelley's Frankenstein monster really a zombie?* But the time wasn't right.

This meeting was about Sam.

Mr. Jones settled back in his chair. "Sam, we'd like you to stay here. We need someone who knows the castle and all its secret spots. Someone who can help ensure our guests have a memorable time."

Dr. Shelley said, "Some people love to be scared."

Sam didn't even think about it. "I'll take the job."

Megan was glad. The castle was a lot closer than Siberia.

Just then, Zach herded Rachel, Brett, and Nurse Karen into the room.

"This is the big cure scene," Zach explained. "It's where Rachel gets brave and saves herself." He went to Rachel and whispered in her ear. He handed her something that Megan couldn't see.

Megan assumed it was a rope or maybe handcuffs. She thought that Rachel was going to capture them and take them to Nurse Karen to be injected with the cure.

"When I say *Action*, Brett and Megan, go outside and attack the house."

"Do not break my window," Mr. Jones said.

"Don't be a spoilsport," Dr. Shelley countered. "Go ahead, kids. Shatter the glass. I'll get it fixed later."

"Already bossing me around?" Mr. Jones asked with a chuckle.

"Forever," Dr. Shelley said. She planned to be infected with the virus and become a zombie herself.

Megan and Brett went back outside and peered through the window. On the count of three, Brett broke the glass with a rock and Megan crawled in through the same window she'd escaped out of hours before.

"Uhhhh-uhhhh," she moaned for the very last time.

Rachel looked terrified, but then as Megan and Brett got closer, her expression became brave. From behind her back, Rachel pulled out the thing that

Zach had given her. It was a dart gun. And before the zombies could shuffle away, Rachel fired darts at them.

"Ouch!" Megan shouted as she fell backward onto the rough woven rug. Something very strange was happening. And it was happening fast. "Zach! What did you do?! I thought we were getting cured. Not shot at."

"Hey!" Brett screamed. "That wasn't in the script. I'm still a zombie, so guess what? I'm going to break the school rules — I'm going to eat *your* brains!" He snarled at Zach.

"That's good, Brett. Keep in character," Zach said. He wasn't scared. He was filming up close now.

Brett struggled to pull the dart out of his rear. He growled, and Megan noticed his teeth were already starting to look normal again.

"I quit!" Megan growled at her brother. "Ouch." She yanked the dart out of her arm, and rubbed it gently.

"You don't have to quit. The movie's a wrap. That scene was totally worth it. Academy Awards, here I come," Zach said. He handed her a mirror. "This is a gift from Happy. She said seven years' bad luck is enough. Don't go for fourteen."

Megan considered hitting Zach over the head with the mirror, but instead, she looked at her reflection.

And there she was.

Megan Murry. Just like she remembered.

"I have a present for you," Megan told Zach on the car ride home. She'd gotten over being shot with the dart when she'd discovered the tip had been soaked in the zombitus cure.

Megan handed Zach the same gift bag he'd given her before she went to Zombie Academy.

"I love presents," Zach said.

Inside was a Zom-B BE A B T-shirt. "I know it's too big," Megan told Zach. "But maybe you could pin it to your wall."

Next was Megan's Zombie Academy red spiral notebook.

"I hope there's something inspirational in there for your next movie," she told him.

The skeleton key. "You never know when you might need it," Megan said.

And finally, at the bottom of the bag was a monster lunch box from Zach's favorite horror movie.

"I bought it online," Megan explained. "You should start a collection."

Zach gave his sister a huge hug. "Uhhhh-uhhhh," he said.

Megan knew exactly what he meant. "Uhhhh-uhhhh to you, too."

ZOMBIE DOG

"Mom, you don't understand," Becky said as her parents did the dishes. "It wasn't just a regular noise." At the table, Jake nodded, his face solemn. They'd been trying to tell their parents about the eerie howl that had come out of the McNally yard, but with one look at her mother's skeptical face Becky knew they hadn't been able to get across how very scary it had been. The kitchen was warm and brightly lit, so normal and safe that it was hard to explain just how *wrong* everything had felt outside.

"It was probably a stray cat in the yard next door," her mother said reasonably. "Let's keep an eye out, and if we see it, we can try to catch it and take it to the animal shelter."

"Bear was really scared, too," Jake said, his face stubborn. "He wouldn't be scared of a stray cat."

Their father's eyebrows rose. "Wait, Bear was there? What was Bear doing when the noise started?"

"He wasn't doing anything!" Becky said, feeling defensive. She folded her arms across her chest. Her parents exchanged a glance. She should have known that they would find a way to make this all about Bear.

"Honey," her mother said firmly, setting down a mug, "we know you love Bear, but he needs to stay off the neighbors' property. And that includes the empty house next door. If he's scaring stray animals over there, he could get hurt."

"*Mom*," Becky said indignantly, "Bear wasn't even over there. He was with us in the yard. He didn't do *anything*. Whatever it was just howled at him for no reason. And you didn't hear this noise. It wasn't any stray cat. It was, like, a banshee or something." She was breathing hard, and she realized as she said it that it was true: The sound felt too eerie to have been made by anything natural.

Her parents stared at her. Then her dad gave a little huffing sigh. "You can't just make up ridiculous stories to cover up Bear's bad behavior," he said.

Becky blinked hard and looked away from her parents. She stared instead at the big poster of different kinds of peppers that her mom had hung over the table, trying to will back tears. They were being so unfair. "Listen," she said, working to keep her voice reasonable, "you don't know all the stuff I've heard about the house next door. Everyone says it's haunted. Or that a mad scientist lived there, or . . . different things. . . ."

The corners of her dad's mouth twitched as if he was stopping himself from laughing, and Becky wanted to scream.

"There's something weird about that house," she told them. "Why do you think it's been empty for so long?"

"The house next door is *haunted*?" Jake asked. He broke into a huge grin. "That's amazing!"

Becky's mom set down the sponge and turned around. "Of course it's not haunted, Jake. Becky, don't try to scare your brother. The house is empty because old Mrs. McNally lives in assisted living now, but she doesn't want to sell it or rent it out," she said matter-of-factly.

"There's always a rational explanation for everything," Becky's father said. "Now, who wants to watch that movie I picked up?"

"I'll make popcorn," her mom said. On her way toward the pantry, she put her hands gently on Becky's shoulders. "I know that moving to a new place can be hard," she said sympathetically, "but making up stories won't help. This is a wonderful house on a terrific street, and you'll adapt."

Becky twitched her shoulders with irritation and her mom let go. "I do love the house," Becky said, turning to look at her mom, "but there's something strange about the house next door."

"I'm sorry, Becky, but that's just not true," her mom said.

"And Becky?" her dad said, and she turned back around to look at him. He pointed one finger at her across the table. "The conversation about Bear's behavior is not over."

In bed that night, Becky couldn't get comfortable. She could hear Bear downstairs in his crate, shifting around restlessly, and occasionally letting out a soft whimper. He didn't like sleeping in the crate, but her parents insisted that he stay in the kitchen at night.

Outside, branches blew against her window. Past them, Becky watched the full moon sailing high in the sky. She buried her face in her pillow and shut her eyes. She had to get some sleep.

Downstairs, Bear barked, one sharp bark. Becky's eyes flew open again, and she listened, wondering if her parents had heard him, but there was no sound from their room. Another whimper came from downstairs, and she threw back her covers and climbed out of bed. Bear was lonely.

Becky tiptoed down the stairs without turning on the light. The moonlight coming through the windows washed across the floor, bright enough to see by.

When Bear saw her, he jumped to his feet, his tail wagging hard enough to rattle the crate.

"Shh, Bear, shh," she said softly. She knelt down on the kitchen floor and put her hands through the bars of the crate to pet him. Bear wagged his tail even harder and licked her fingers enthusiastically. "You need to go to sleep, boy," she told him in a whisper. "If you wake up Mom and Dad, they're not going to be happy with us."

As Becky started to stand up, Bear gave her a sad look, his big brown eyes wide, and her heart melted.

"Okay, honey," she whispered. "You can come with me just for tonight." Bear whuffed happily at her as she unlatched the crate. "Shh," she said, grabbing hold of his collar.

Once they got upstairs, Bear heaved himself up onto her bed, turned in a half circle to get comfortable, and stretched out. After a moment, Becky climbed into the bed next to him. Bear immediately snuggled next to her, resting his furry head against her shoulder. Becky closed her eyes and tried again to fall asleep.

A few minutes later, Bear began to snore. Becky's eyes snapped open. Gradually, Becky became aware of a constant, low whining noise. It occasionally stopped, but always started again. Was Bear whining in his sleep? No, his breathing was regular and steady, interspersed with soft, deep snores. The whining was coming from somewhere else.

Outside, maybe? Becky climbed out of bed. The floor was cold against her feet as she moved hesitantly toward the window, following the sound. When she looked out the window, the scene was shadowy, but lit by the full moon.

Maybe there was a stray cat or lost dog in the McNally yard, as Becky's parents had suggested. She peered down into the patch of the yard next door that she could see through her window. The whining was a little louder now, and irregular. Not the sound of the porch swing creaking or a branch rubbing against the house, but definitely some kind of animal. Becky pressed her forehead against the cold window pane, trying to see.

Something moved in the shadows on the other side of the fence.

It was a huddled shape below one of the evergreen trees in the McNally yard. As Becky watched, it moved a little farther into the moonlight.

Was it a cat, after all? It seemed like it might be cat-size, but the shape didn't seem quite right. The tail was too short, the body looked off somehow. It was moving stiffly, not with the smooth glide of a hunting cat.

The animal raised its head and looked right at Becky. Its eyes flashed a sick, glowing yellowish green.

Instinctively, she moved back, away from the window. Had it seen her? Her heart pounded and she felt like she couldn't catch her breath. Panic bubbled inside her. She didn't know why, but she didn't want the creature to know she was there.

POISON APPLE BOOKS

The Dead End

This Totally Bites!

Miss Fortune

Now You See Me...

Midnight Howl

Her Evil Twin

Curiosity Killed the Cat

At First Bite

THRILLING.
BONE-CHILLING.
THESE BOOKS
HAVE BITE!